THE POET

X

A NOVEL BY
ELIZABETH ACEVEDO

First published in USA 2018 by HarperCollins Children's Books
First published in Great Britain 2018
by Egmont UK Limited
The Yellow Building, 1 Nicholas Road, London W11 4AN

Published by arrangement with HarperCollins Children's Books,
a division of HarperCollins Publishers, New York, New York, USA

Text copyright © 2018 Elizabeth Acevedo

ISBN 978 1 4052 9146 0

A CIP catalogue record for this title is available from the British Library

68775/1

Printed and bound in Great Britain by the CPI Group

Stay safe online. Any website addresses listed in this book are correct at the time
of going to print. However, Egmont is not responsible for content hosted by third
parties. Please be aware that online content can be subject to change and websites
can contain content that is unsuitable for children. We advise that all children
are supervised when using the internet.

Advance Praise for  THE POET X

"A story that will slam the power of poetry
and love back into your heart."
—LAURIE HALSE ANDERSON,
author of National Book Award finalists *Speak* and *Chains*

"Elizabeth Acevedo crackles with energy and snaps with
authenticity and voice. Every poem in this stunningly addictive
and deliciously rhythmic verse novel begs to be read aloud.
Xiomara is a protagonist who readers will cheer for at every
turn. As X might say, Acevedo's got bars. Don't pass this one by."
—JUSTINA IRELAND, author of *Dread Nation*

"I devoured this magnificent work of art. Elizabeth Acevedo
gets everything right, bringing the magic of the verse novel to
stunning new heights. A glorious achievement. This is a story
about what it means to be a writer and how to survive when
it feels like the whole world's turned against you. Required
reading for everybody alive today."
—DANIEL JOSÉ OLDER,
author of the Shadowshaper Cypher series

"Though vivid with detail about family, love, and culture, *The Poet X* is more of an exploration of when the poet becomes the poem. Xiomara teeters between verbosity and restraint, shape and form, rewriting and sharing. Most important, the poet (and poem) searches for the freedom to stand on her own. Acevedo delivers an incredibly potent debut."

—JASON REYNOLDS,
author of National Book Award finalist *Ghost*

"In *The Poet X*, Acevedo skillfully sculpts powerful, self-contained poems into a masterpiece of a story, and has amplified the voices of girls en el barrio who are equal parts goddess, saint, warrior, and hero."

—IBI ZOBOI, author of *American Street*

To Katherine Bolaños and my former students
at Buck Lodge Middle School 2010–2012,
and all the little sisters yearning to see themselves:
this is for you

PART I

In the Beginning

Was the Word

Friday, August 24
Stoop-Sitting

The summer is made for stoop-sitting
and since it's the last week before school starts,
Harlem is opening its eyes to September.

I scope out this block I've always called home.

Watch the old church ladies, chancletas flapping
against the pavement, their mouths letting loose a train
of island Spanish as they spread he said, she said.

Peep Papote from down the block
as he opens the fire hydrant
so the little kids have a sprinkler to run through.

Listen to honking cabs with bachata blaring
from their open windows
compete with basketballs echoing from the Little Park.

Laugh at the viejos—my father not included—
finishing their dominoes tournament with hard slaps
and yells of *"Capicu!"*

Shake my head as even the drug dealers posted up
near the building smile more in the summer, their hard scowls
softening into glue-eyed stares in the direction

of the girls in summer dresses and short shorts:

"Ayo, Xiomara, you need to start wearing dresses like that!"
"Shit, you'd be wifed up before going back to school."
"Especially knowing you church girls are all freaks."

But I ignore their taunts, enjoy this last bit of freedom,
and wait for the long shadows to tell me
when Mami is almost home from work,

when it's time to sneak upstairs.

Unhide-able

I am unhide-able.

Taller than even my father, with what Mami has always said
was "a little too much body for such a young girl."
I am the baby fat that settled into D-cups and swinging hips
so that the boys who called me a whale in middle school
now ask me to send them pictures of myself in a thong.

The other girls call me conceited. Ho. Thot. Fast.
When your body takes up more room than your voice
you are always the target of well-aimed rumors,
which is why I let my knuckles talk for me.
Which is why I learned to shrug when my name was replaced
     by insults.

I've forced my skin just as thick as I am.

Mira, Muchacha

Is Mami's favorite way to start a sentence
and I know I've already done something wrong
when she hits me with: "Look, girl . . ."

This time it's "Mira, muchacha, Marina from across the street
told me you were on the stoop again talking to los vendedores."

Like usual, I bite my tongue and don't correct her,
because I hadn't been talking to the drug dealers;
they'd been talking to me. But she says she doesn't
want any conversation between me and *those* boys,
or any boys at all, and she better not hear about me hanging out
like a wet shirt on a clothesline just waiting to be worn
or she would go ahead and be the one to wring my neck.

"Oíste?" she asks, but walks away before I can answer.

Sometimes I want to tell her, the only person in this house
who isn't heard   is me.

Names

I'm the only one in the family
without a biblical name.
Shit, Xiomara isn't even Dominican.

I know, because I Googled it.
It means: One who is ready for war.

And truth be told, that description is about right
because I even tried to come into the world
in a fighting stance: feet first.

Had to be cut out of Mami
after she'd given birth
to my twin brother, Xavier, just fine.
And my name labors out of some people's mouths
in that same awkward and painful way.

Until I have to slowly say:
See-oh-MAH-ruh.
I've learned not to flinch the first day of school
as teachers get stuck stupid trying to figure it out.

Mami says she thought it was a saint's name.
Gave me this gift of battle and now curses
how well I live up to it.

My parents probably wanted a girl who would sit in the pews
wearing pretty florals and a soft smile.
They got combat boots and a mouth silent
until it's sharp as an island machete.

The First Words

Pero, tú no eres fácil

is a phrase I've heard my whole life.
When I come home with my knuckles scraped up:

Pero, tú no eres fácil.

When I don't wash the dishes quickly enough,
or when I forget to scrub the tub:

Pero, tú no eres fácil.

Sometimes it's a good thing,
when I do well on an exam or the rare time I get an award:

Pero, tú no eres fácil.

When my mother's pregnancy was difficult,
and it was all because of me,

because I was turned around
and they thought that I would die

or worse,
that I would kill her,

so they held a prayer circle at church
and even Father Sean showed up at the emergency room,

Father Sean, who held my mother's hand
as she labored me into the world,

and Papi paced behind the doctor,
who said this was the most difficult birth she'd been a part of

but instead of dying I came out wailing,
waving my tiny fists,

and the first thing Papi said,
the first words I ever heard,

"Pero, tú no eres fácil."
You sure ain't an easy one.

Mami Works

Cleaning an office building in Queens.
Rides two trains in the early morning
so she can arrive at the office by eight.
She works at sweeping, and mopping,
emptying trash bins, and being invisible.
Her hands never stop moving, she says.
Her fingers rubbing the material of plastic gloves
like the pages of her well-worn Bible.

Mami rides the train in the afternoon,
another hour and some change to get to Harlem.
She says she spends her time reading verses,
getting ready for the evening Mass,
and I know she ain't lying, but if it were me
I'd prop my head against the metal train wall,
hold my purse tight in my lap, close my eyes
against the rocking, and try my best to dream.

Tuesday, August 28
Confirmation Class

Mami has wanted me to take the sacrament
of confirmation for three years now.

The first year, in eighth grade, the class got full
before we could sign up, and even with all her heavenly pull

Mami couldn't get a spot for Twin and me.
Father Sean told her it'd be fine if we waited.

Last year, Caridad, my best friend, extended her trip in D.R.
right when we were supposed to begin the classes,

so I asked if I could wait another year.
Mami didn't like it, but since she's friends with Caridad's mother

Twin went ahead and did the class without me.

This year, Mami has filled out the forms,
signed me up, and marched me to church

before I can tell her that Jesus feels like a friend
I've had my whole childhood

who has suddenly become brand-new;
who invites himself over too often, who texts me too much.

A friend I just don't think I need anymore.
(I know, I know . . . even writing that is blasphemous.)

But I don't know how to tell Mami that this year,
it's not about feeling unready,
it's about knowing that this doubt has already been confirmed.

God

It's not any one thing
    that makes me wonder
        about the capital G.O.D.

About a holy trinity
    that don't include the mother.
        It's all the things.

Just seems as I got older
    I began to really see
        the way that church

treats a girl like me differently.
    Sometimes it feels
        all I'm worth is under my skirt

and not between my ears.
    Sometimes I feel
        that turning the other cheek

could get someone like my brother killed.
    Sometimes I feel
        my life would be easier

if I didn't feel like such a debt
        to a God
              that don't really seem

to be   out here   checking   for me.

"Mami," I Say to Her on the Walk Home

The words sit in my belly,
and I use my nerves
like a pulley to lift
them out of my mouth.

"Mami, what if I don't
do confirmation?
What if I waited a bit for—"

But she cuts me off,
her index finger a hard exclamation point
in front of my face.

"Mira, muchacha,"
she starts, "I will
feed and clothe no heathens."

She tells me I *owe* it to
God and myself to devote.
She tells me this country is too soft
and gives kids too many choices.

She tells me if I don't confirm here
she will send me to D.R.,

where the priests and nuns know
how to elicit true piety.

I look at her scarred knuckles.
I know exactly how she was taught
faith.

When You're Born to Old Parents

Who'd given up hope for children
and then are suddenly gifted with twins,
you will be hailed a miracle.
An answered prayer.
A symbol of God's love.
The neighbors will make the sign of the cross
when they see you,
thankful you were not a tumor
in your mother's belly
like the whole barrio feared.

When You're Born to Old Parents, Continued

Your father will never touch rum again.
He will stop hanging out at the bodega
where the old men go to flirt.
He will no longer play music
that inspires swishing or thrusting.
You will not grow up listening
to the slow pull of an accordion
or rake of the güira.

Your father will become "un hombre serio."
Merengue might be your people's music
but Papi will reject anything
that might sing him toward temptation.

When You're Born to Old Parents, Continued Again

Your mother will engrave
your name on a bracelet,
the words *Mi Hija* on the other side.

This will be your favorite gift.
This will become a despised shackle.
Your mother will take to church
like a dove thrust into the sky.
She was faithful before, but now
she will go to Mass every single day.

You will be forced to go with her
until your knees learn the splinters of pews,
the mustiness of incense,
the way a priest's robe tries to shush silent
all the echoing doubts
ringing in your heart.

The Last Word on Being Born to Old Parents

You will learn to hate it.

No one, not even your twin brother,
will understand the burden
you feel because of your birth;

your mother has sight for nothing
but you two and God;
        your father seems to be serving
a penance, an oath of solitary silence.

Their gazes and words
are heavy with all the things
they want you to be.

It is ungrateful to feel like a burden.
It is ungrateful to resent my own birth.
I know that   Twin and I are miracles.

Aren't we reminded every single day?

Rumor Has It,

Mami was a comparona:
stuck-up, they said, head high in the air,
hair that flipped so hard
that shit was doing somersaults.

Mami was born en La Capital,
in a barrio of thirst buckets
who wrote odes to her legs,
but the only man Mami wanted
was nailed to a cross.

Since she was a little girl
Mami wanted to wear a habit,
wanted prayer and the closest
thing to an automatic heaven admission
she could get.

Rumor has it, Mami was forced to marry Papi;
nominated by her family
so she could travel to the States.
It was supposed to be a business deal,
but thirty years later, here they still are.

And I don't think Mami's ever forgiven Papi
for making her cheat on Jesus.

Or all the other things he did.

Tuesday, September 4
First Confirmation Class

And I already want to pop the other kids right in the face.
They stare at me like they don't got the good sense—
or manners—I'm sure their moms gave them.

I clip my tongue between my teeth
and don't say nothing, don't curse them out.
But my back is stiff and I'm unable to shake them off.

And sure, Caridad and I are older
but we know most of the kids from around the way,
or from last year's youth Bible study.

So I don't know why they seem so surprised to see us here.
Maybe they thought we'd already been confirmed,
with the way our mothers are always up in the church.

Maybe because I can't keep the billboard frown off my face,
the one that announces I'd rather be anywhere but here.

Father Sean

Leads the confirmation class.
He's been the head priest at La Consagrada Iglesia
as long as I been alive,
which means he's been around forever.

Last year, during youth Bible study, he wasn't so strict.
He talked to us in his soft West Indian accent,
coaxing us toward the light.
Or maybe I just didn't notice his strictness
because the older kids were always telling jokes,
or asking the important questions
we really wanted to know the answers to:
"Why should we wait for marriage?"
"What if we want to smoke weed?"
"Is masturbation a sin?"

But confirmation class is different.
Father Sean tells us we're going to deepen
our relationship with God.
"Of your own volition you will accept him into your lives.
You will be sealed with the gift of the Holy Spirit.
And this is a serious matter."

That whole first class,
I touch my tongue to the word *volition*,
like it's a fruit I've never tasted
that's already gone sour in my mouth.

Haiku

Father Sean lectures
I wait for a good moment
whispering to C:

Boys

X: You make out with any boys while you were in D.R.?

C: Girl, stop. Always talking about some boys.

X: Well if you didn't kiss nobody, why you all red in the face?

C: Xiomara, you know I didn't kiss no boy.
Just like I know you didn't.

X: Don't look at me like that. *I'm* not proud of the fact
that I still ain't kiss nobody. It's a damn shame, we're almost
sixteen.

C: Don't say *damn*, Xiomara. And don't roll your eyes at me
either. You won't even be sixteen until January.

X: I'm just saying, I'm ready to stop being a nun. Kiss a boy,
shoot, I'm ready to creep with him behind a stairwell and let him
feel me up.

C: Oh God, girl. I really just can't with you.
Here, here's the Book of Ruth. Learn yourself some virtue.

X: Tsk, tsk. You gonna talk about this in a church,
then take his name in vain. Ouch!

C: Keep talking mess. I'm going to do more than pinch you.
I don't know why I missed you.

X: Maybe because I make you laugh more than your
stuffy-ass church mission friends?

C: I can't with you. Now, stop worrying about kissing and boys.
I'm sure you'll figure it out.

Caridad and I Shouldn't Be Friends

We are not two sides of the same coin.
We are not ever mistaken for sisters.

We don't look alike, don't sound alike.
We don't make no damn sense as friends.

I curse up a storm and am always ready to knuckle up.
Caridad recites Bible verses and promotes peace.

I'm ready to finally feel what it's like to like a boy.
Caridad wants to wait for marriage.

I'm afraid of my mother so I listen to what she says.
Caridad genuinely respects her parents.

I should hate Caridad. She's all my parents want in a daughter.
She's everything I could never be.

But Caridad, Twin, and I have known each other since diapers.
We celebrate birthdays together, attended Bible

camp sleepovers with each other, spend Christmas Eve
at each other's houses.

She knows me in ways I don't have to explain.
Can see one of my tantrums coming a mile off,

knows when I need her to joke, or when I need to fume,
or when I need to be told about myself.

Mostly, Caridad isn't all extra goody-goody in her judgment.
She knows all about the questions I have,

about church, and boys, and Mami.
But she don't ever tell me I'm wrong.

She just gives me one of her looks,
full of so much charity, and tells me that she knows

I'll figure it all out.

Questions I Have

Without Mami's Rikers Island Prison–like rules,
I don't know who I would be
when it comes to boys.

It's so complicated.
For a while now I've been having all these feelings.
Noticing boys more than I used to.

And I get all this attention from guys
but it's like a sancocho of emotions.

This stew of mixed-up ingredients:
partly flattered they think I'm attractive,
partly scared they're only interested in my ass and boobs,
and a good measure of Mami-will-kill-me fear sprinkled on top.

What if I like a boy too much and become addicted to sex
like Iliana from Amsterdam Ave.?
Three kids, no daddy around,
and baby bibs instead of a diploma hanging on her wall.

What if I like a boy too much and he breaks my heart,
and I wind up angry and bitter like Mami,
walking around always exclaiming how men ain't shit,
even when my father and brother are in the same room?

What if I like a boy too much
and none of those things happen . . .
they're the only scales I have.

How does a girl like me figure out the weight
of what it means to love a boy?

Wednesday, September 5
Night before First Day of School

As I lie in bed,
thinking of this new school year,

I feel myself
stretching my skin apart.

Even with my Amazon frame,
I feel too small for all that's inside me.

I want to break myself open
like an egg smacked hard against an edge.

Teachers always say
that each school year is a new start:

but even before this day
I think I've been beginning.

Thursday, September 6
H.S.

My high school is one of those old-school structures
from the Great Depression days, or something.

Kids come from all five boroughs, and most of us bus or train,
although since it's my zone school, I can walk to it on a nice day.

Chisholm H.S. sits wide and squat, taking up half a block,
redbrick and fenced-in courtyard with ball hoops and benches.

It's not like Twin's fancy genius school: glass, and futuristic.
This is the typical hood school, and not too long ago

it was considered one of the worst in the city:
gang fights in the morning and drug deals in the classroom.

It's not like that anymore, but one thing I know for sure
is that reputations last longer than the time it takes to make them.

So I walk through metal detectors, and turn my pockets out,
and greet security guards by name, and am one of hundreds

who every day are sifted like flour through the doors.
And I keep my head down, and I cause no waves.

I guess what I'm trying to say is, this place is a place,
neither safe nor unsafe, just a means, just a way to get closer

to escape.

Ms. Galiano

Is not what I expected.
Everyone talks about her
like she's super strict
and always assigning
the toughest homework.

So I expected someone older,
a buttoned-up, floppy-haired,
suit-wearing teacher,
with glasses sliding down her nose.

Ms. Galiano is young, has on bright colors,
and wears her hair naturally curly.
She's also little—like, for real petite—
but carries herself big, know what I mean?
Like she's used to shouldering her way
through any assumptions made about her.

Today, I have her first-period English,
and after an hour and fifteen minutes of icebreakers,
where we learn one another's names
(Ms. Galiano pronounces mine right on the first try),
she gives us our first assignment:

"Write about the most impactful day of your life."

And although it's the first week of school,
and teachers always fake the funk the first week,
I have a feeling Ms. Galiano
actually wants to know my answer.

***Rough Draft of Assignment 1—Write about the most impactful
day of your life.***

The day my period came, in fifth grade, was just that,
the ending of a childhood sentence.
The next phrase starting in all CAPS.

No one had explained what to do.
I'd heard older girls talk about "that time of the month"
but never what someone was supposed to use.

Mami was still at work when I got home from school and went
to pee, only to see my panties smudged in blood. I pushed Twin off
the computer and Googled "Blood down there."

Then I snuck money from where Mami hides it beneath the pans,
bought tampons that I shoved into my body
the way I'd seen Father Sean cork the sacramental wine.

It was almost summer. I was wearing shorts.

I put the tampon in wrong. It only stuck up halfway
and the blood smeared between my thighs.

When Mami came home I was crying.
I pointed at the instructions;

Mami put her hand out but didn't take them.
Instead she backhanded me so quick she cut open my lip.

"Good girls don't wear tampones.
Are you still a virgin? Are you having relations?"

I didn't know how to answer her, I could only cry.
She shook her head and told me to skip church that day.
Threw away the box of tampons, saying they were for cueros.
That she would buy me pads. Said eleven was too young.
That she would pray on my behalf.

I didn't understand what she was saying.
But I stopped crying. I licked at my split lip.
I prayed for the bleeding to stop.

Final Draft of Assignment 1 (What I Actually Turn In)

Xiomara Batista

Friday, September 7

Ms. Galiano

The Most Impactful Day of My Life, Final Draft

When I turned twelve my twin brother saved up enough lunch money to get me something fancy: a notebook for our birthday. (I got him some steel knuckles so he could defend himself, but he used them to conduct electricity for a science project instead. My brother's a genius.)

The notebook wasn't the regular marble kind most kids use. He bought it from the bookstore. The cover is made of leather, with a woman reaching to the sky etched on the outside, and a bunch of motivational quotes scattered like flower petals throughout the pages. My brother says I don't talk enough so he hoped this notebook would give me a place to put my thoughts. Every now and then, I dress my thoughts in the clothing of a poem. Try to figure out if my world changes once I set down these words.

This was the first time someone gave me a place to collect my thoughts. In some ways, it seemed like he was saying that my thoughts were important. From that day forward I've written every single day. Sometimes it seems like writing is the only way I keep from hurting.

The Routine

Is the same every school year:
I go straight home after school
and since Mami says that I'm "la niña de la casa,"
it's my job to help her out around the house.

So after school I eat an apple—my favorite snack—
wash dishes, and sweep.
Dust around Mami's altar to La Virgen María
and avoid Papi's TV if he's home
because he hates when I clean in front of it
while he's trying to watch las noticias or a Red Sox game.

It's one of the few things Twin and I argue about,
how he never has to do half the cleaning shit I do
but is still better liked by Mami.

He helps me when he's home, folds the laundry
or scrubs the tub. But he won't get in trouble if he doesn't.

I hear one of Mami's famous sayings in my ear,
"Mira, muchacha, life ain't fair,
that's why we have to earn our entrance into heaven."

Altar Boy

Twin is easier for Mami to understand. He likes church.
As much of a science geek as he is,
he doesn't question the Bible the way that I do.

He's been an altar boy since he was eight,
could quote the New Testament—in Spanish and English—
since he was ten, leads discussions at Bible study
even better than the priest. (No disrespect to Father Sean.)

He even volunteered at the Bible camp this summer
and now that school's started he'll miss
the Stations of the Cross dioramas his campers made
from Popsicle sticks, the stick figure drawings
of Mary in the manger, the mosaic made of marbles
that he hung in the window of our room,

the one that I threw out this afternoon while I was cleaning,
watched it fall between the fire escape grates. For a second,
it caught the sun in a hundred colors

                        until it smashed against the street.

I'll apologize to Twin later. Say it was an accident.
He'll forgive me. He'll pretend to believe me.

Twin's Name

For as long as I can remember
I've only ever called my brother "Twin."

He actually *is* named after a saint,
but I've never liked to say his name.

It's a nice name, or whatever,
even starts with an *X* like mine,

but it just doesn't feel like the brother I know.
His real name is for Mami, teachers, Father Sean.

But *Twin*? Only I can call him that,
a reminder of the pair we'll always be.

More about Twin

Although Twin is older by almost an hour—
of course the birth got complicated when it was my turn—
he doesn't act older. He is years softer than I will ever be.

When we were little, I would come home
with bleeding knuckles and Mami would gasp
and shake me: "¡Muchacha, siempre peleando!
Why can't you be a lady? Or like your brother?
He never fights. This is not God's way."

And Twin's eyes would meet mine
across the room. I never told her
he didn't fight because my hands
became fists for him. My hands learned
how to bleed when other kids
tried to make him into a wound.

My brother was birthed a soft whistle:
quiet, barely stirring the air, a gentle sound.
But I was born all the hurricane he needed
to lift—and drop—those that hurt him to the ground.

Tuesday, September 11
It's Only the First Week of Tenth Grade

And high school is already a damn mess.
In ninth grade you are in between.
No longer in junior high,
but still treated like a kid.

In ninth grade you are always frozen
between trying not to smile or cry,
until you learn that no one cares about
what your face does, only what your hands'll do.

I thought tenth grade would be different
but I still feel like a lone shrimp
in a stream where too many are searching
for someone with a soft shell
to peel apart and crush.

Today, I already had to curse a guy out
for pulling on my bra strap,
then shoved a senior into a locker
for trying to whisper into my ear.

"Big body joint," they say,
"we know what girls like you want."

And I'm disgusted at myself
for the slight excitement
that shivers up my back

at the same time that I wish
my body could fold into the tiniest corner
for me to hide in.

How I Feel about Attention

If Medusa was Dominican
and had a daughter, I think I'd be her.
I look and feel like a myth.
A story distorted, waiting for others to stop
and stare.

Tight curls that spring like fireworks
out of my scalp. A full mouth pressed hard
like a razor's edge. Lashes that are too long
so they make me almost pretty.

If Medusa
was Dominican and had a daughter, she might
wonder at this curse. At how her blood
is always becoming some fake hero's mission.
Something to be slayed, conquered.

If I was her kid, Medusa would tell me her secrets:
how it is that her looks stop men
in their tracks   why they still keep on coming.
How she outmaneuvers them when they do.

Saturday, September 15
Games

With one of our last warm-weather Saturdays
Twin, Caridad, and I go to the Goat Park
on the Upper West Side.

Outside of ice-skating when we were little,
neither Twin nor I are particularly athletic,
but Caridad loves "trying new social activities"
and this week it's a basketball tournament.

The three of us have always been tight like this.
And although we're different,
since we were little we've just clicked.

Sometimes Twin and Caridad are the ones
who act more like twins,
but our whole lives we've been friends, we've been family.

Already we feel the chill that's biting at the edge of the air.
It will be hoodie weather soon,
and then North Face weather after that,
but today it's still warm enough for only T-shirts,
and I'm kind of glad for it because the half-naked ball players?
  They're FINE.

Running around in ball shorts, and no tees,
their muscles sweaty, their skin flushed.
I lean against the fence and watch them
race up and down the court.

Caridad is paying attention to the ball movement,
but Twin's staring as hard as I am at one of the ballers.
When he catches me looking Twin pretends to clean his glasses
    on his shirt.

When the game is over (the Dyckman team won),
we shuffle away with the crowd,
but just as we get to the gate one of the ball players,
a young dude about our age, stops in front of me.

"Saw you looking at me kind of hard, Mami."

Damn it. Recently, I haven't been able to stop looking.
At the drug dealers, the ball players, random guys on the train.
But although I like to look, I hate to be seen.

All of a sudden I'm aware of how many boys
on the ball court have stopped to stare at me.
I shake my head at the baller and shrug.
Twin grabs my arms and begins pulling me away.
The baller steps to Twin.

"Oh, is this your girl? That's a lot of body
for someone as small as you to handle.
I think she needs a man a little bigger."

When I see his smirk, and his hand cupping his crotch,
I break from Twin's grip, ignore Caridad's intake of breath,
and take a step until I'm right in homeboy's face:

"Homie, what makes you think you can 'handle' me,
when you couldn't even handle the ball?"

I suck my teeth as the smile drops off his face;
the dudes around us start hooting and hollering in laughter.
I keep my chin up high and shoulder my way through the crowd.

After

It happens when I'm at bodegas.
It happens when I'm at school.
It happens when I'm on the train.
It happens when I'm standing on the platform.
It happens when I'm sitting on the stoop.
It happens when I'm turning the corner.
It happens when I forget to be on guard.
It happens all the time.

I should be used to it.
I shouldn't get so angry
when boys—and sometimes
grown-ass men—
talk to me however they want,
think they can grab themselves
or rub against me
or make all kinds of offers.
But I'm never used to it.
And it always makes my hands shake.
Always makes my throat tight.
The only thing that calms me down
after Twin and I get home
is to put my headphones on.
To listen to Drake.

To grab my notebook,
and write, and write, and write
all the things I wish I could have said.
Make poems from the sharp feelings inside,
that feel like they could
carve me wide
open.

It happens when I wear shorts.
It happens when I wear jeans.
It happens when I stare at the ground.
It happens when I stare ahead.
It happens when I'm walking.
It happens when I'm sitting.
It happens when I'm on my phone.
It simply never stops.

Okay?

Twin asks me if I'm okay.
And my arms don't know
which one they want to become:
a beckoning hug or falling anvils.

And Twin must see it on my face.
This love and distaste I feel for him.
He's older (by a whole fifty minutes)
and a guy, but never defends me.

Doesn't he know how tired I am?
How much I hate to have to be so
sharp tongued and heavy-handed?

He turns back to the computer
and quietly clicks away.
And neither of us has to say
we are disappointed in the other.

Sunday, September 16
On Sunday

I stare at the pillar
in front of my pew
so I don't have to look
at the mosaic of saints,
or the six-foot sculpture
of Jesus rising up from behind
the priest's altar.
Even with the tambourine
and festive singing,
these days, church seems
less party and more prison.

During Communion

Ever since I was ten,

I've always stood with the other parishioners
at the end of Mass to receive the bread and wine.

But today, when everybody thrusts up from their seats
and faces Father Sean, my ass feels bolted to the pew.

Caridad slides past, her right brow raised in question,
and walks to the front of the line.

Mami elbows me sharply and I can feel
her eyes like bright lampposts shining on my face,

but I stare straight ahead, letting the stained glass
of la Madre María blur into a rainbow of colors.

Mami leans down: "Mira, muchacha, go take God.
Thank him for the fact that you're breathing."

She has a way of guilting me compliant.
Usually it works.

But today, I feel the question
sticking to the roof of my mouth like a wafer:

what's the point of God giving me life
if I can't live it as my own?

Why does listening to his commandments
mean I need to shut down my own voice?

Church Mass

When I was little,
I loved Mass.
The clanging tambourines
and guitar.
The church ladies
singing hymns
to merengue rhythms.
Everyone in the pews
holding hands and clapping.
My mother, tough at home,
would cry and smile
during Father Sean's
mangled Spanish sermons.

It's just when Father Sean
starts talking about the Scriptures
that everything inside me
feels like a too-full,
too-dirty kitchen sink.

When I'm told girls
Shouldn't. Shouldn't. Shouldn't.
When I'm told
To wait. To stop. To obey.

When I'm told not to be like
Delilah. Lot's Wife. Eve.

When the only girl I'm supposed to be
was an impregnated virgin
who was probably scared shitless.
When I'm told fear and fire
are all this life will hold for me.

When I look around the church
and none of the depictions of angels
or Jesus or Mary, not one of the disciples
look like me: morenita and big and angry.

When I'm told to have faith
in the father   the son
in men   and men are the first ones

to make me feel so small.

That's when I feel like a fake.
Because I nod, and clap, and "Amén" and "Aleluya,"
all the while feeling like this house   his house
is no longer one I want to rent.

Not Even Close to Haikus

Mami's back is a coat hanger.
Her anger made of the heaviest wool.
It must keep her so hot.

*

"Mira, muchacha,
when it's time to take the body of Christ,
don't you *ever* opt out again."

*

But I can hold my back like a coat hanger, too.
Straight and stiff and unbending
beneath the weight of her hard glare.

*

"I don't want to take
the bread and wine, and Father Sean says
it should always and only be done with joy."

*

Mami gives me a hard look.

I stare straight ahead.

It's difficult to say who's won this round.

Holy Water

"I just don't know about that girl,"
Mami loud-whispers to Papi.
They never think that Twin and I can hear.

But since they barely say two words
to each other unless it's about us or dinner,
we're always listening when they speak

and these flimsy Harlem walls
barely muffle any sound.

"Recently, she's got all kinds of devils inside of her.
They probably come from you.
I've talked to Padre Sean and he said
he'll talk to her at confirmation class."

And I want to tell Mami:
Father Sean talking to me won't help.
That incense makes bow tie pasta of my belly.
That all the lit candles beckon like fingers
that want to clutch around my throat.
That I don't understand her God anymore.

I hear Papi shushing her quiet.
"It's that age. Teenage girls are overexcited.
Puberty changes their mind. Son locas."

And since Papi knows more
about girls than she does
she stays silent at his reply.

I don't know if it's prayer to hope
that soon my feelings will drown me faster
than the church's baptismal water.

Papi was a mujeriego.
That he would get drunk at the barbershop
and touch the thigh of any woman
who walked too close.

They say his tongue was slick
with compliments and his body
was like a tambor with the skin
stretched too tight.

They say Papi was broken,
that he couldn't get women pregnant,
so he tossed his seeds to the wind,
not caring where they landed.

They say Twin and I saved him.
That if it wasn't for us
Mami would have kicked him to tomorrow
or a jealous husband would have shanked him dead.

They say Papi used to love to dance
but now he finally has a spine
that allows him to stand straight.
They say we made it so.

On Papi

You can have a father who lives with you.
Who every day eats at the table
and watches TV in the living room

and snores through the whole night
and grunts about the bills, or the weather,
or your brother's straight As.

You can have a father who works for Transit Authority,
and reads *El Listín Diario*,
and calls back to the island every couple of months
to speak to Primo So-and-So.

You can have a father who, if people asked,
you had to say lived with you.
You have to say is around.

But even as he brushes by you
on the way to the bathroom
he could be gone as anybody.

Just because your father's present
doesn't mean he isn't absent.

All Over a Damn Wafer

As repentance for not participating in communion last time,
Mami makes me go
to evening Mass with her every evening this week,
even the days that aren't confirmation class.

When Communion time comes
I stand in line with everyone else
and when Father Sean places the Eucharist
onto my tongue I walk away,
kneel in my pew,
and spit the wafer into my palm
when I'm pretending to pray.

I can feel the hot eyes of the Jesus statue
watching me hide the wafer beneath the bench,
where his holy body will now feed the mice.

Monday, September 17
The Flyer

"Calling all poets!"

The poster is printed
on regular white computer paper.
The bare basics:

Spoken Word Poetry Club
Calling all poets, rappers, and writers.
Tuesdays. After school.
See Ms. Galiano in room 302 for details.

It's layered behind other more colorful
and bigger-lettered announcements
but it still makes me stop
halfway down the staircase,
as kids late to class
try their best to accidentally
make me topple down the stairs.
But I'm rooted to the spot,
a new awareness buzzing over the noise.

This poster feels personal,
like an engraved invitation
mailed directly to me.

After the Buzz Dies Down

I crumple the flyer in my backpack.
Balled and zipped up tight.
Tuesdays I have confirmation class.

Not a chance Mami's gonna let me out of that.
Not a chance I want anyone hearing my work.

Something in my chest flutters like a bird
whose wings are being gripped still

by the firmest fingers.

Tuesday, September 18
Aman

After two weeks of bio review,
safety lessons, and blahzayblahblah—
we're finally starting real work.
A boy, Aman, is assigned as my lab partner.

I saw him around last year,
but this is our first class together.

He shifts at the two-person desk we share
and his forearm touches mine.

After a moment, I shift on purpose,
liking how my arm brushes against his.
I pull away quickly.

The last thing I need is for someone to see me
trying to holla at a dude in the middle of class.
Then I'll really be known as fast.

But it's like his forearm brush changed everything.

Now I notice how I'm taller than him by a couple of inches.
How full his mouth is. How he has a couple of chin hairs.

How quiet he is. How he peeks at me from under his lashes.
Near the end of class, as we both stare at the board
I let my arm rest against his. It seems safe, our silence.

Whispering with Caridad Later That Day

X: There's this boy at school . . .

C: This is why your mom should have sent you
with me to St. Joan's.

X: Are you kidding? Half those girls
end up pregnant before graduating.

C: No exageres, Xio.
And we're going to get in trouble.
We're supposed to be annotating this verse.

X: You and I could break this verse down in our sleep.
It's not wrong to think a boy is fine, you know.

C: It's wrong to lust, Xio. You know it's a sin.

X: We're humans, not robots. Even our parents lusted once.

C: That's different. They were married.

X: You don't think they lusted before the aisle?
Girl, bye. Anyways, there's a boy at school.
He's cute. His arm . . . is warm.

C: I don't even want to know what you mean by that.
Is that code for something? Stop being fresh.

X: Caridad, you always trying to protect me
from my dirty mind . . . of warm arms.

C: Sometimes I think I'm the only one
trying to protect you from yourself.

What Twin Be Knowing

As I'm getting ready for sleep, I'm surprised
to see the crumpled poetry club flyer
neatly unfolded and on my bed.
It must have fallen out of my bag.

Without looking up from the computer screen,
Twin says in barely a whisper,

"This world's been waiting
for your genius a long time."

My brother is no psychic, no prophet,
but it makes me smile,
this secret hope we share,
that we are both good enough
for each other and maybe the world, too.

But when he goes to brush his teeth,
I tear the flyer into pieces before Mami can find it.
Tuesdays, for the foreseeable future,
belong to church. And any genius I might have
belongs only to me.

Sharing

Although Twin and I are super different,
people find it strange how much we share.
We shared the same womb, the same cradle,
and our whole lives the same room.

Mami wanted to find a bigger apartment,
told Papi we should move to Queens,
or somewhere far from Harlem,
where we could each have our own room.

But apparently, although Papi had changed
he still stood unmoved.
Said everything we could want was here.
And sharing a room wouldn't kill us.

And it hasn't.
Except. I once heard a rumor
that goldfish have an evolutionary gene
where they'll only develop as big as the tank they're put into.

They need space to stretch. And I wonder if
Twin and I are keeping each other small.
Taking up the space that would have let the other grow.

Questions for Ms. Galiano

I'm one of the first students in English class the next day.
And although I promised myself I would keep my lips
stapled together when Ms. Galiano asks me how I'm doing,
the words trip and twist their ankles
trying to rush out my mouth: "Soyourunthepoetryclubright?"

She doesn't laugh. Cocks her head, and nods.
"Yes, we just started it this year. Spoken Word Poetry Club."

And my face must have been all kinds of screwed-up confused
because she tries to explain how spoken word is performed poetry,
but it all sounds the same to me . . . except one is memorized.

"It might be easier if I showed you.
I'll pull a clip up as today's intro to class.
Are you thinking of joining the club?"

I shake my head no. She gives me that look again,
when someone who doesn't know you is sizing you up
like you're a broken clock and they're trying to translate the ticks.

Spoken Word

When class starts Ms. Galiano projects a video:
a woman onstage, her voice quiet,
then louder and faster like an express train picking up speed.

The poet talks about being black, about being a woman,
about how beauty standards make it seem she isn't pretty.
I don't breathe for the entire three minutes

while I watch her hands, and face,
feeling like she's talking directly to me.
She's saying the thoughts I didn't know anyone else had.

We're different, this poet and I. In looks, in body,
in background. But I don't feel so different
when I listen to her. I feel heard.

When the video finishes, my classmates,
who are rarely excited by anything, clap softly.
And although the poet isn't in the room

it feels right to acknowledge her this way,
even if it's only polite applause;
my own hands move against each other.

Ms. Galiano asks about the themes and presentation style
but instead of raising my hand I press it against my heart
and will the chills on my arms to smooth out.

It was just a poem, Xiomara, I think.

But it felt more like a gift.

Wait–

Is this what Ms. Galiano thinks
I'm going to do in her poetry club?
She mentioned competition,
and I know slam is just that,
but she can't think that I,
who sits silently in her classroom,
who only speaks to get someone off my back,
will ever get onstage
and say any of the things I've written,
out loud, to anybody else.

She must be out her damn mind.

Holding a Poem in the Body

Tonight after my shower
instead of staring at the parts of myself
I want to puzzle-piece into something else,
I watch my mouth memorize one of my poems.

Even though I don't ever plan on letting anyone hear it,
I think about that poetry video from class . . .

I let the words shape themselves hard on my tongue.
I let my hands pretend to be punctuation marks
that slash, and point, and press in on each other.
I let my body finally take up all the space it wants.

I toss my head, and screw up my face,
and grit my teeth, and smile, and make a fist,
and every one of my limbs
is an actor trying to take center stage.

And then Mami knocks on the door,
and asks me what I'm in here reciting,
that it better not be more rap lyrics,
and I respond, "Verses. I'm memorizing verses."
I know she thinks I mean Bible ones.

I hide my notebook in my towel before heading to my room and comfort myself with the fact that I didn't actually lie.

J. Cole vs. Kendrick Lamar

Now that we're doing real labs
Aman and I are forced to speak.
Mostly we mumble under our breath
about measurements and beakers,
but I can't forget what I told Caridad:

I want to get to know him.

I ask him if he has the new J. Cole album.
Shuffle papers as I wait for him to answer.
Aman signs his name beneath mine on the lab report.
The bell rings, but neither of us moves.
Aman straightens and for the first time his eyes lock onto mine:

"Yeah, I got Cole, but I rather the Kendrick Lamar—
we should listen to his new album together sometime."

Asylum

When my family first got a computer,
Twin and I were about nine.

And while Twin used it to look up astronomy discoveries
or the latest anime movies,

I used it to stream music.
Flipping the screen from music videos

to Khan Academy tutorials
whenever Mami walked into the room.

I fell in love with Nicki Minaj,
with J. Cole, with Drake and Kanye.

With old-school rappers like
Jay Z and Nas and Eve.

Every day I searched for new songs,
and it was like applying for asylum.

I just needed someone to help me escape
from all the silence.

I just needed people saying words
about all the things that hurt them.

And maybe this is why Papi stopped listening to music,
because it can make your body want to rebel. To speak up.

And even that young I learned music can become a bridge
between you and a total stranger.

What I Tell Aman:

"Maybe. I'll let you know."

Dreaming of Him Tonight

A boy's face in my hands,
but he's nearly a man.
Memories of Mami's words
almost lash my fingers away
but still I brush upward,
against the grain and prickle
and bristle of a light beard at his jaw.
His cheekbones rise like a sun;
the large canvas of a forehead.
A nose that takes space.
This is a face that doesn't apologize
for itself.

The boy moves his body closer to mine
and I can feel his hands
drop down from my waist to my hips
then brushing up toward these boobs I hate
that I now push at him like an offering,
his hands move so close, our faces move closer—
and then my phone alarm rings,
waking me up for school.

In my dreams his is a mouth that knows
more than curses and prayer. More

than bread and wine. More
than water. More
than blood.
More.

Thursday, September 20
The Thing about Dreams

When I get to school
I know I won't be able to look Aman in the face.

You can't dream about touching a boy
and then look at him in real life
and not think he's going to see
that dream like a face full of makeup
blushing up your cheeks.

But even though I'm nervous
when I get to bio, the moment
I sit next to him I calm down.
Like my dream has given me
an inside knowledge
that takes away my nerves.

"I'd love to listen to Kendrick.
Maybe we could do it tomorrow?"

Date

This doesn't count as a date.
Or even anything sinful.
Just two classmates
meeting up after school
to listen to music.

So I try not to freak out
when Aman agrees
to our non-date.

Mami's Dating Rules

Rule 1. I can't date.

Rule 2. At least until I'm married.

Rule 3. See rules 1 and 2.

Clarification on Dating Rules

The thing is,
my old-school
Dominican parents
Do. Not. Play.

Well, mostly Mami.
I'm not sure Papi
has any strong opinions,
or at least none he's ever said.

But Mami's been telling me
early as I can remember
I can't have a boyfriend
until I'm done with college.

And even then,
she got strict rules
on what kind of boy
he better be.

And Mami's words
have always been
scripture set in stone.
So I already know

going to a park
alone with Aman
might as well be
the eighth deadly sin.

But I can't wait
to do it anyway.

Friday, September 21
Feeling Myself

All last night, I held the secret of meeting Aman
like a candle that could too easily be blown out.

Any time Mami said my name, or Twin looked in my direction,
I waited for them to ask what I was hiding.

This morning, I iron my shirt. A for-sure sign I'm scheming
since I hate to iron.

But no one says anything about the shirt,
or my new shea butter–scented lip balm.

And when I slide my jeans up my hips and shimmy into them
my legs feel powerful beneath my hands

and I smile over my shoulder at my bubble butt in the mirror.

PART ❙❙

And the Word

Was Made Flesh

Smoke Parks

Because I wouldn't go to his house
(not that he asked me to!),
we both know that our secret friendship
can take place only in public.

Every Friday our school has a half day for professional development,
and today Aman and I shuffle to the smoke park nearby.
I've never smoked weed,
but I think Aman does sometimes after school;
I smell it on his sweater, and know the crowd he chills with.

But today the park is ours
and we sit on a bench with more
than our forearms "accidentally" rubbing.
His fingers brush against my face
as he places one of his earbuds in for me.

I can smell his cologne
and I want to lean in but I'm
afraid he'll notice I'm sniffing him.
For a moment, the only thing I can hear
is my own heart loudly pumping
in my ears.

I close my eyes and let myself
find in music what I've always searched for:
a way away.

After an hour, when the album clicks off
and Aman tugs on my hand to pull me up from the bench
I hold on. Link my fingers with his for just a moment.
And walk to the train feeling truly thankful
that this city has so many people to hide me.

I Decided a Long Time Ago

Twin is the only boy I will ever love.
I don't want a converted man-whore like my father
so the whole block talks about my family and me.

I don't want a pretty boy,
or a superstar athlete, more in love with himself
than anyone else.

I wouldn't even date a boy like Twin,
thinking people are inherently good,
always seeing the best in them.

But I have to love Twin.
Not just because we're blood, but because
he's the best boy I know.

He is also the worst twin in the world.

Why Twin Is a Terrible Twin

He looks nothing like me.
He's small. Scrawny.
Straight-up scarecrow skinny.
(I must have bullied him in Mami's belly
because it's clear I stole all the nutrients.)

He wears glasses because he's afraid
of poking an eye out by using contacts.
He doesn't even try to look cool, or match.

He is, in fact, the worst Dominican:
doesn't dance, his eyebrows connect slightly,
he rarely gets a shape-up, and he'd rather read
than watch baseball. And he hates to fight.
Didn't even wrestle with me when we were little.

I've gotten into too many shove matches
trying to make sure Twin walked away
with his anime collection.

My brother ain't no stereotype, that's for sure.

Why Twin Is a Terrible Twin, for Real

Twin is a genius.
Full sentences at eight months old,
straight As since pre-K,
science experiments and scholarships
to space camp since fifth.

This also means we haven't been
in the same grade since we were really little,
and then he got into a specialized high school,
so his book smarts meant
I couldn't even copy his homework.

He is an award-winning bound book,
where I am loose and blank pages.
And since he came first, it's his fault.
And I'm sticking to that.

Why Twin Is a Terrible Twin (Last and Most Important Reason)

He has no twin intuition!
He doesn't get sympathy pains.
He doesn't ever randomly know
that I had a bad day or that I need help.
In fact, he rarely lifts his eyes from the
page of a Japanese comic or the computer screen
long enough to know that I'm here at all.

But Why Twin Is Still the Only Boy I'll Ever Love

Because although speaking to him
is like talking to a scatterbrained saint,
every now and then, he'll say, in barely a mumble,
something that shocks the shit out of me.
Today he looks up from his textbook and blinks.

"Xiomara, you look different.
Like something inside of you has shifted."

I stop breathing for a moment.
Is my body marked by my afternoon with Aman?
Will Mami see him on me?

I look at Twin, the puzzled smile on his face;
I want to tell him he looks different, too—
maybe the whole world looks different
just because I brushed thighs with a boy.
But before I get the words out
Twin opens his big-ass mouth:

"Or maybe it's just your menstrual cycle?
It always makes you look a little bloated."

I toss a pillow at his head and laugh.
"Only you, Twin. Only you."

Sunday, September 23
Communication

Aman and I exchanged numbers to talk about lab work
but when I leave Mass I'm surprised to see
he's messaged me.

A: So what did you think of the Kendrick?

And because Mami is angry-whispering
at me for sitting out the sacrament again
(I'll do another bid of Mass all week if I have to),
I cage my squeal behind my teeth.
I type a quick response:

X: It was cool. We should listen to something else next time.

And his response is almost immediate:

A: Word.

About A

Every time I think about Aman
poems build inside me
like I've been gifted a box of metaphor Legos
that I stack and stack and stack.
I keep waiting for someone to knock them over.
But no one at home cares about my scribbling.

Twin: oblivious—although happier than he usually looks.
Mami: thinking I'm doing homework.
Papi: ignoring me as usual . . . aka being Papi.
Me: writing pages and pages about a boy
and reciting them to myself like a song, like a prayer.

Monday, September 24
Catching Feelings

In school things feel so different.
Ms. Galiano asks me about the Spoken Word Poetry Club,
and I try to pretend I forgot about it.

But I think she can tell by my face
or my shrug that I've been secretly practicing.
That I spend more time writing poems
or watching performance videos on YouTube
than I do on her assignments.

At lunch, I sit with the same group I sat with last year,
a table full of girls that want to be left alone.
I find comfort in apples and my journal,
as the other girls read books over their lunch trays,
or draw manga, or silently text boyfriends.
Sharing space, but not words.

In bio, when I lower my ass into the seat
next to Aman, I wonder if I should sit slower,
or faster, if I should write neater,
or run a fingertip across his knuckles
when Mr. Bildner isn't looking.

Instead Aman and I pass notes on scrap paper
talking about our days, our parents,
our favorite movies and songs,
and the next time we'll go to the smoke park.

If my body was a Country Club soda bottle,
it's one that has been shaken and dropped
and at any moment it's gonna pop open
and surprise the whole damn world.

Notes with Aman

A: You ever messed with anyone in school?

X: Nah, never really be into anyone.

A: We not cute enough for you?

X: Nope. Ya ain't.

A: Damn. Shit on my whole life!

X: You just want me to say you cute.

A: Do you think I am?

X: I'm still deciding ☺

What I Didn't Say to Caridad in Confirmation Class

I wanted to tell her that if Aman were a poem
he'd be written slumped across the page,
sharp lines, and a witty punch line
written on a bodega brown paper bag.

His hands, writing gently on our lab reports,
turned into imagery,
his smile the sweetest unclichéd simile.

He is not elegant enough for a sonnet,
too well-thought-out for a free write,
taking too much space in my thoughts
to ever be a haiku.

Lectures

"Mira, muchacha,"—

(I'm not sure if your eyes
can roll so hard in your head
that a stranger could use them
as a pair of dice, but if they can
someone just bad lucked on snake eyes)—

"when I was waiting for you
I saw you whispering to Caridad
in the middle of your class.
Do not let yourself get distracted
so that you lead yourself and others
from la palabra de dios."

And although the night has cooled down
the fading summer heat,
sweat breaks out on my forehead,
my tongue feels swollen,
dry and heavy with all I can't say.

Ms. Galiano's Sticky Note on Top of Assignment 1

Xiomara,

*Although you say you're only "dressing your thoughts
in poems," I've found a lot of your work is quite poetic. I
wonder why you don't consider yourself a poet?*

*I love that your brother gave you a notebook you still use.
You really should come to the poetry club. I have a feeling
you'd get a lot out of it.*

—G

Sometimes Someone Says Something

And their words are like the catch of a gas stove,
the *click, click* while you're waiting
for it to light up and then flame big and blue . . .
That's what happens when I read Ms. Galiano's note.

A bright light lit up inside me.

But now I crumple up the note and assignment
and throw them out in the cafeteria trash can.
Because every day the idea of poetry club is like Eve's apple:
something you can want but can't have.

Friday, September 28
Listening

Today when Aman and I sit on the bench
I wait for him to pass me his headphones,
but he plays with my fingers instead.

"No music today, X.
Instead I want to hear you.
Read me something."

And I instantly freeze.
Because I never, *never* read my work.
But Aman just sits patiently.

And with my heart thumping
I pull my notebook out.
"You better not laugh."

But he just leans back and closes his eyes.
And so I read to him.
Quietly. A poem about Papi.

My heart pumps hard in my chest,
and the page trembles when I turn it,
and I rush through all the words.

111

And when I'm done I can't look at Aman.

I feel as naked as if I'd undressed before him.

But he just keeps fiddling with my fingers.

"Makes me think of my mother being gone.

You got bars, X. I'm down to listen to them anytime."

Mother Business

Aman and I don't really talk about our families like that.
I know the rules. You don't ask about people's parents.
Most folks got only one person at home,
and that person isn't even always the egg or the sperm donor.
But I feel like I said too much and too little about Papi.
And now I want to know more about Aman's family.

"Can you tell me about your moms? Why is she gone?"

His mouth looks zipped-up silent.
We are quiet for a while and there's no noise to cover my shiver.
Even lost in his thoughts, Aman notices,
tucks my hand clasped with his inside his jacket pocket.
I'm glad the cold breeze is a good excuse
for why my cheeks go pink. He finally looks at me.
His eyes trying to read something in my face.

I don't expect him to ever answer.

And Then He Does

"My moms was a beautiful woman.
She and Pops married when they were teens.
He came here first, then sent for us.

I was old enough when I came here
that I can remember Trinidad:

the palm tree behind my grandma's house,
the taste of backyard mangoes,
the song in the voice every time someone spoke.

I was young enough to learn how my accent
could be rolled tight between my lips
until this country smoked it out
into that clipped 'good-accented English.'

My mother never came, you know.
She would call every day at first
and always tell me the same thing,
she 'was handling affairs.' 'We'll be together soon.'

She calls every year on my birthday.
I've stopped asking her when she's coming.
Pops and I get on just fine.

I've learned not to be angry.
Sometimes the best way to love someone
is to let them go."

Warmth

Aman and I walk from our park
but instead of walking straight to the train
we skip the station, then the next.
We are silent the whole walk.
Without words we are in agreement
that we'll walk as far as we can this way:
my hand   held   in his   held
in his coat pocket. Each of us keeping
the other warm against the quiet chill.

Tuesday, October 9
The Next Couple of Weeks

Pass by like an express train
and before I know it,
October has cooled the air,
and we're all pressed into
hoodies and jackets.

I try to avoid Ms. Galiano,
who always reminds me
I'm more than welcome
to join poetry club.

Aman and I don't share
a lunch period but we walk together
to the train after school,
listening to music or just enjoying the quiet.

I think we both want to do more,
but I'm still too shy and he's still too . . . Aman.
Which means he never presses too hard
and I have to wonder if he's being respectful
or isn't feeling me like that.

But he wouldn't be hanging out with me so much
if he wasn't feeling me, right?
And although I still want to stay seated during Communion,
I get up every time, put the wafer in my mouth
then slip it beneath the pew.
My hands shaking less and less every time I do.

The hardest thing has been Tuesdays.
I sit in confirmation class
knowing I could be in poetry club instead,
or writing, or doing anything other
than trying to unhear everything Father Sean says.

And I do a good job of pretending.

At least until the day
I open my usually silent mouth
and decide to ask Father Sean
about Eve.

Eve,

Father Sean explains,
could have made a better choice.

Her story is a parable
to teach us how to deal with temptation.

Resist the apple.

And for some reason,
either because of what I'm learning

in school and in real life,
I think it all just seems like bullshit.

So I say so. Out loud. To Father Sean.
Next to me Caridad goes completely still.

"I Think the Story of Genesis Is Mad Stupid"

"God made the Earth in seven days?
Including humans, right?
But in biology we learned
dinosaurs existed on Earth
for millions of years
before other species . . .
unless the seven days is a metaphor?
But what about humans evolving
from apes? Unless Adam's creation
was a metaphor, too?
And about this apple,
how come God didn't explain
why they couldn't eat it?
He gave Eve curiosity
but didn't expect her to use it?
Unless the apple is a metaphor?
Is the whole Bible a poem?
What's *not* a metaphor?
Did any of it *actually* happen?"

I catch my breath. Look around the room.
Caridad is bright red.
The younger kids are silent,
watching like it's a WWE match.

And Father Sean's face has turned
hard as the marble altar.

"Why don't you and I talk
after class, Xiomara?"

As We Are Packing to Leave

C: Xiomara, if Father Sean says something to your moms
it's going to be a hot mess—

X: So what? Aren't we supposed to be curious
about the things that we're told?

C: Listen. Don't come at me like that, Xiomara.
I'm just trying to help you.

X: I know, I know. But . . . they were just questions.
Aren't priests obligated to confidentiality?

C: That wasn't a confession, Xiomara.

X doesn't say: Wasn't it?

Father Sean

Tells me
I seem distracted in confirmation class.

Tells me
perhaps there is something I'd like to discuss besides Eve.

Tells me
it's normal to be curious about the world.

Tells me
Catholicism invites curiosity.

Tells me
I should find solace in a forgiving religion.

Tells me
the church is here for me if I need it.

Tells me
maybe I should have a conversation with my mother.

Tells me
open and honest dialogue is good for growth.

Tells me

a lot of things but none of them an answer to anything I asked.

Answers

After Father Sean's lecture, he seems to expect answers from me.

I stare at the picture behind his desk.
It's him in a boxing ring holding a pair of gold gloves.

"You still fight, Father Sean?"

He cocks his head at me, and his lips quirk up a bit.

"Every now and then I get into a ring to stay in shape.
I definitely don't fight as much as I used to.
Not every fight can be fought with gloves, Xiomara."

I stand. I tell Father Sean I won't ask about Eve again.
I leave church before *he* asks *me* something I can't answer.

Rough Draft Assignment 2–Last Paragraphs of My Biography

And that's how Xiomara,
bare-knuckled, fought the world
into calling her correctly by her name,
into not expecting her to be a saint,
into respecting her as a whole grown-ass woman.

She knew since she was little,
the world would not sing her triumphs,
but she took all of the stereotypes
and put them in a chokehold
until they breathed out the truth.

Xiomara may be remembered
as a lot of things: a student,
a miracle, a protective sister,
a misunderstood daughter,

but most importantly,
she should be remembered
as always working to become
the warrior she wanted to be.

Final Draft of Assignment 2 (What I Actually Turn In)

Xiomara Batista

Monday, October 15

Ms. Galiano

Last Paragraphs of My Biography, Final Draft

Xiomara's accomplishments amounted to several key achievements. She was a writer who went on to create a nonprofit organization for first-generation teenage girls. Her center helped young women explain to their parents why they should be allowed to date, and go away for college, and move out when they turned eighteen . . . also, how to discover what they wanted to do in life. It was an organization that helped thousands of young women, and although they never built a statue outside the center (she would have hated that) they did hang a super-blown-up selfie of her in the main office.

Since her parents were distraught that the neighborhood had changed, that there were no more Latino families and the bodegas and sastrería were all closed down, Xiomara used her earnings to buy them a house in the Dominican Republic. Although she was never married and didn't have children, Xiomara was happy with a big pit bull and a brownstone in Harlem not too far from the neighborhood where she was raised. Her twin brother lived down the street.

Hands

In bio
Aman's hand has started
finding mine inside the desk.

I hope I don't sweat
as his finger fiddles
across my palm.

I wonder if he's nervous
like me. If he's frontin'
like me.

Pretending I've played
with someone's hand,
and done even more.

And even though
I've dreamed about him before,
there's something different

about touching a guy
in real life. In the flesh.
Inside a classroom. More than once.

His hand lighting a match
inside my body.

Fingers

In bed at night
my fingers search
a heat I have no name for.

Sliding into a center,
finding a hidden core,
or stem, or maybe   the root.

I'm learning how to caress
and breathe at the same time.

How to be silent
and feel something grow
inside me.

And when it all builds up,
I sink into my mattress.
I feel such a release. Such a relief.

I feel such a shame
settle like a blanket
covering me head to toe.

To make myself feel this way
is a dirty thing, right?
Then why does it feel so good?

Tuesday, October 16
Talking Church

"So you go to church a lot, right?"
Aman asks as we walk to the train.

And any words I have
suicide-jump off my tongue.
Because this is it.

Either he's going to think
I'm a freak of the church
who's too holy to do anything,

or he's going to think I'm
a church freak trying to get it on
with the first boy who tries.

"X?"

And I try to focus on that,
how much I love this new nickname.
How it's such a small letter
but still fits all of me.

"Xiomara?"
I finally turn to look at him.

"Yeah. My moms is big into church
and I go with her and to confirmation classes."

"So your moms is big into the church,
but you, what are you big into?"

And I let loose the breath that I was holding.
And before I know I'm going to say them
the words have already escaped my mouth.

"You already know I'm into poetry."

And he nods. Looks at me and seems to decide something.
"So what's your stage name, Xiomara?"

And I'm so glad he's changed the subject.
That I answer before I think:
"I'm just a writer . . . but maybe I'd be the Poet X."

He smiles. "I think that fits you perfectly."

Swoon

In science we learned
that thermal conductivity
is how heat flows through
some materials better than others.
But who knew words,
when said by the right person,
by a boy who raises your temperature,
move heat like nothing else?
Shoot a shock of warmth
from your curls to your toes?

Telephone

Twin doesn't ask who I'm texting
so late into the night that the glow
of my phone is the only light
in the whole apartment.

And I don't offer to tell him
or to hide my texting
beneath my blanket.

I've never been superfriendly,
and Caridad is the only person
we really talk to, unless I'm working
on a class project or something.

But now I have Aman,
sweet and patient Aman,
who sends me Drake lyrics
that he says remind him of me

and asks me to whisper him poems in return.
Who never grows tired of my writing
and always asks for one more.

Twin doesn't ask who I'm texting.
Though I know he's wondering
because I'm wondering who he's been texting, too.

The reason why he's smiling more now.
And giggles in the dark,
the glow of his phone letting me know

we both have secrets to keep.

Over Breakfast

Twin is singing underneath his breath
as he pours milk into his cereal.

I watch him as I sip on a cup of coffee.
He slices up an apple and gives me half.

He knows they're my favorite,
but I'm surprised he's being so thoughtful.

"Twin, you been smiling more lately.
This person got a name?"

And my words make the smile
slip and slide right off his face.

He shakes his head at me,
pushes his cereal away.

He plays with the tablecloth.
"Is that why *you* been smiling so much?"

And to cover my blush,
I gulp down the last of my coffee.

"I'm just happy; you know what we should plan?
Our scary movie date for Halloween. You and me."

And we both say at the same time:
"And Caridad."

Angry Cat, Happy X

C: Girl, this angry cat meme reminded me of you.

X: Smh. Ur dumb. I was just about to text you.
Scary movie Halloween date?

C: Duh! How you doing? How's that boy you feeling?

X: I'm good . . . He's fine.

C: Why ". . ."?

X: I know you don't approve.

C: Xio, I just don't want you getting in trouble.
But I like seeing you happy . . . Like *this* happy cat meme!

Friday, October 19
About Being in Like

The smoke park is empty again.
And I'm so glad we finally
have another half day.

The afternoon stretches before us.
No Mami to call me. She's still at work.
Twin's genius school runs on a different schedule.
Caridad never texts during class.

It's just me and Aman
and his hand brushing my cheek
to insert an earbud.

"You ever smoked a blunt?"

I shake my head.

"Word. Drake is better when you lit.
But we can listen to him anyways."

And so I shut my eyes,
pressing my shoulder closer to his
as he settles his iPhone between us,
as he settles his hand on my thigh.

Music

for A

Placing my head in the crook of your neck
makes me happy   to be alive.
Eyes closed   hands clasped.
Don't breathe   and maybe
we will live   like this forever.
It be gibberish   but everything
you whisper   sounds like poetry.
I   missed   you.

This was supposed to be a question.

Not a poem   confession   or whatever it's become.
I just wanted   to know if   you would listen
with me   to the sound   of our heartbeats.

Tuesday, October 23
Ring the Alarm

The day that becomes THE DAY
starts real regular. Same schedule,
and nothing changed 'til last-period bio.

It's the first Tuesday
since "the Eve episode"
and with thirty minutes left of school
a fire alarm goes off.

Mr. Bildner sighs and stops the PowerPoint
that was showing us how Darwin
figured out finches.

Aman squeezes my hand beneath the desk
and stands. Slings his bag across his shoulders
(he never puts it in his locker).

Before I know what I'm saying
the words skip like small rocks out my mouth:
"We should go to the park."

They sink in silence. He cocks his head.
"You know Bildner's going to take attendance
if this is a false alarm?"

The class lines up to exit
and as we scrunch together
my ass bumps Aman's front.
I don't move away.

I whisper over my shoulder,
"We should still go."
Aman's finger pulls on one of my curls.

"I didn't know you liked Drake enough
to get caught cutting."

I lean back against him,
feel his body pressed against mine.
"Drake isn't the one that I like."

The Day

We are side by side
sitting on our park bench.

Aman slides his arm around my shoulder
and pulls me closer to him.

Today there are no headphones,
no music, just us.

He brushes his lips across my forehead
and I shiver from something other than cold.

His fingers tip up my chin;
my hands instantly get sweaty and I can't look at him

so I stare at his eyebrows: cleanly arched,
no stray hairs, prettier than any girl's,

and I lean in trying to figure out
if he waxes or threads.

Then he's leaning in too and I know
I have one moment to make a decision.

So I press my lips to his.

His mouth is soft against mine.
Gently, he bites my bottom lip.

And then his tongue slides in my mouth.
It's messier than I thought it'd be.

He must notice, because
his tongue slows down.

And my heart is one of Darwin's finches learning to fly.

Wants

As much as boys and men
have told me all of the things
they would like to do to my body,
this is the first time I've actually wanted
some of those things done.

At My Train Stop

My train pulls slowly into the station
so I take my hand out of Aman's.
He looks at me with a question on his face
and I can feel the heat creep up my cheeks.

He's asking me something
but I can't hear a word he's saying
because I keep getting distracted by his lips
and the fact that I now know how they taste.

"X, did you hear me?
I'll text you later. Maybe we can go out this weekend?
To Reuben's Halloween party?"

I hop off the train without giving him an answer,
without waving at him through the window.
With too many things to say and nothing to say at all.

What I Don't Tell Aman

I can't date.
I can't be seen on my block with boys.
I can't have a boy call my cell phone.
I can't hold hands with a boy.
I can't go to his house.
I can't invite him to mine.
I can't hang out with him and his friends.
I can't go to the movies with any boy other than Twin.
I can't go to teen night at the club.
I can't have a boyfriend.

I can't fall in love.

Whenever we text late at night
I avoid mentioning making plans.
I tell him "I just want to live in the moment."

Because I don't want to tell him all the things I can't do.

But I also shouldn't kiss a boy in the smoke park . . .
and yet, I did that, too.

Kiss Stamps

Later, when I walk into confirmation class
I know I'm wearing Aman's kiss
like a bright red sweater.
Anyone who looks at me
will know I know what it means to want.
In that way. Because I didn't want to stop kissing.
And we didn't.
Until his hands moved under
my shirt and I jumped at the chill.
Maybe I jumped at something else.
Guilt? How fast we're moving?
I don't know, but I knew it was time to stop.
But I didn't want to.
I mean, I guess I did.
It's confusing   to know
you shouldn't be doing something,
that it might go too far,
but still wanting to do it anyway.
I don't whisper with Caridad,
or make eye contact with anyone,
or question Father Sean,
or look at the cross
bearing an all-knowing God who, if he exists,
saw everything, *everything*
that happened in the smoke park.

And how much I enjoyed it.

The Last Fifteen-Year-Old

Okay. I know. It's not that deep to kiss a guy.
It's just a kiss, some tongue, little kids kiss all the time,
probably not with tongue (that'd be weird).

Boys have wanted to kiss me
since I was eleven, and back then I didn't want to kiss them.
And then it was grown-ass boys, or legit men,
giving me sneaky looks, and Mami told me I'd have to pray extra
so my body didn't get me into trouble.

And I knew then what I'd known since my period came:
my body was trouble. I had to pray the trouble out
of the body God gave me. My body was a problem.
And I didn't want any of these boys to be the ones to solve it.
I wanted to forget I had this body at all.

So when everyone in middle school was playing truth or dare,
or whatever other excuse to get their first kiss,
I was hiding in big sweaters, I was hiding in hard silence,
trying to turn this body into an invisible equation.

Until now. Now I want Aman to balance my sides,
to leave his fingerprints all over me. To show all his work.

Concerns

Father Sean asks me if things are going well?
And for a second, I think he knows about the kiss.
That through some divine premonition
or psychic ability . . . he knows.

But then I see him glance at the altar
at the covered chalice full of wine,
the plate holding the soft circles of the body of Christ.

I'm fine. I'm fine. I'm fine. I don't say.
I just shrug. And look anywhere else.

"We all doubt ourselves sometimes," he tells me.
I look him straight in the eye: "Even you?"

He gives me a small smile that makes him look younger . . .
You ever look at someone that you've known
your whole life and it's almost like their face
reconfigures itself right in front of your eyes?

Father Sean's smile makes him look different
and I can imagine the young man he once was.

"Especially me. My whole life I wanted to be a boxer,
an athlete. I thought my body was my way out

of the terrible circumstances I lived in—instead
it was the body of Christ that got me out,
but sometimes I miss my island. My family.
My mother died and I didn't get there in time to say good-bye.
We all doubt ourselves and our path sometimes."

I want to say I'm sorry, to bring back the young Father Sean smile
but instead I merely nod.

Some things don't need words.

What Twin Knows

"Twin, you know Father Sean's mom died?"

Twin looks up distracted from his phone,
where his fingers have been rapidly texting.
I try to read over his shoulder but he flips
it screen-down on the desk.

"Yeah, she died three summers ago.
Why you bringing that up?"

And I don't know how I didn't know.
How I didn't notice Father Sean gone,
or notice the person who took over his sermons.
Have I been checked out of church for that long?

I don't ask Twin any of these questions.
He's already back on his phone.

"Who you been texting so much lately?"

The question shoulders past my lips
and I stop with one of my headphones
halfway into my ear.
Twin has never kept secrets from me.

154

His thumbs go still on his phone.
And he gives me a long, long look.

"Xiomara, we don't have to do this, right?
Maybe with everyone else we need to explain.
But we both know we're messing around
and that Mami and Papi will kill us if they find out."

And I want to nod my head, and shake it no at the same time.
Our parents always say that as la niña de la casa
expectations for me are different than for Twin.
If he brought a girl home they would probably applaud him.

I don't know what they would do
        if the person he brought home was not a girl.

Hanging Over My Head

The next couple of days,
I wait for Aman
to bring up the Halloween party.
But he holds my hand in bio,
walks me to the train in the afternoons,
kisses me good-bye before I exit to the platform,
and doesn't mention the party again.
Maybe he doesn't want me to go anymore?

Friday, October 26
Friday

Is usually my favorite day of the week.
But this morning I got a text from Aman
that flavored my whole day sour:

A: Got a doc appointment.
Not coming to school.
See ya at the party?

And I know it's going to be
a long two days between
now and when I'll see him again.

Unless I figure out a way . . .

Black & Blue

What kind of twin am I
who didn't even notice
when my own brother
comes home with a black eye?

I mean I noticed, but not until
I heard Mami yelling at him tonight
while he was getting
something from the fridge.

"¿Y eso, muchacho? ¿Quién te pegó?
¿No me digas que fue Xiomara?"

But I'm already halfway to the kitchen,
then pulling his chin from her grip,
inspecting his eye myself.
I don't say a word to him
and Twin's face flinches in my hand.

"No es nada. It's nothing.
It was just a misunderstanding."

And although he's answering her,
his eyes are pleading with me.

"Yeah, looks like some asshole
misunderstood your face
for a punching bag."

Mami looks back and forth between us,
probably only catching
every other word of the English,
but even she knows   when it's a twin thing.

Tight

I'm so heated
with Twin
for not telling me
someone at school
was bothering him
that I stop speaking.

It's a silent Friday.

On Saturday
I wake up
with a different feeling
tightening my belly.
I want to go to the party.
I want to see Aman.

The boys in my life
will drive me crazy
one way or another.

Saturday, October 27
Excuses

X: Hey, so, would you be really mad
if I didn't go with you and Twin to the movies—

C: Is this about the boy?

X: Kinda . . . I'm telling my mother I'm hanging out with you.
I'll be home at the same time as you both.

C: Is he making you lie to your mother?

X: He's not making me do anything. Except meet him at a party.

C: Be safe, Xio . . . Your brother's been acting strange lately.
Are you sure he's coming to the movies?

X: Yeah . . . he has a lot going on. Don't ask about his black eye.
But he'll be there.

C: Black eye? Did you hit him, Xiomara?

X: Why does everyone keep asking that? No!
But I'm going to hit the dude who did.

C: Don't make it any worse.
You know your brother hates confrontation.

X: Yeah, yeah, yeah. Thanks for not being mad at me.

C: Just don't get pregnant. I'm too young to be a godmother.

Costume Ready

I leave with Twin to "the movies"
although we go in different directions
once we get to the corner.

He walks toward Caridad's house,
and I walk to the train station
on my way up to the Heights.

A block away from Reuben's house
I sneak into a Starbucks bathroom
and put on green eye shadow, fluff my curls.

Tug on the hem of Twin's Green Lantern tee
(it fits tight around my boobs and shows some midriff.
I'm glad Mami didn't ask to see what I had on under my jacket.)

and voilà—a half-assed superhero costume.

Reuben's House Party

When I get to the address in Washington Heights
I know I'm too early.

There are only a handful of people there,
who, like me, made bootleg attempts at a costume.

I see a couple of people I know from school,
but no one I would hang out with.

This is a party crowd: the loudest, the boldest,
the ones who smoke during the school day,
and drink their parents' mamajuana on the weekend.

Someone hands me a cup of fruity drink
but I put it down on the TV stand, lean against the wall.

I don't look at the clock blinking from the DVD player;
I don't look at my phone.
I've got an alarm set so I know when to leave.

For now I just listen to the noise, to the music,
ignore the stares of a group of boys by the speakers.

When someone brushes my hand I brace myself, tighten my jaw,
but when I turn it's Aman. Playing with my fingers, smiling.

"I didn't think you were going to make it.
Do you want something to drink?"

I shake my head no. And take in his outfit. He went all out.
Face painted green, waves spinning, T-shirt stuffed with something,

all his lean self trying to look like the Hulk.
I can't hold my laughter and he only smiles wider.

"We are meant to be," he whispers.
"We both chose green superheroes."

Someone lowers the lights.
Aman tugs on my hand. "Dance with me?"

One Dance

When Aman asks, my heart starts thumping.
Because this isn't bachata or merengue or something
with coordinated steps and distance.

This song is the kind you get close for.
I push off the wall and Aman shifts in front of me,
his hands holding my hips.

I close my eyes and wipe my sweaty palms
on the back of his shirt; we're pressed against each other,
swaying, his mouth near my neck.

The shoulder pads under his costume
give me something to hold on to,
and I'm glad we have at least the padding between us.

Then his leg is between mine
and we're dancing exactly the way people do
in music videos.

Like if they weren't wearing clothes
they'd be . . . you know.
I can feel all of him. Not as scrawny as I thought.

When the song is over,
another reggae one comes on and Aman
rotates so now he's behind me.

His body grinds against mine,
and it feels so good.
I push away from him.

"I need some air."

Stoop-Sitting ... with Aman

Outside of Reuben's building,
the Heights is on fire.
People dressed in all kinds of costumes,
laughing, and yelling, and singing,
you would think it was morning and not 9:30 p.m.

Aman holds my hand in his
but every time I look at him
I'm afraid my cheeks will burst
bright red, so I don't.

And then he drops the bomb:
"I don't live too far from here."
And I don't know if he means
he wants me to go to his house,
or if he's just talking to talk.

"Isn't your father home?"
I really hope his father's home.
Aman shakes his head.
Tells me his father works tonight.

I pull my hand from his.
I can't stop my fingers

from trembling.
I don't have to fake when I tell him

I don't feel great.
That I should get home
and make tea or something.
I get up to leave, but before I do,
Aman tugs at my hand:

"Read me a poem, X?
I want to remember your voice
when I think about tonight."

And then he's grinning again
and pulls me down beside him.

Convos with Caridad

X: I'm on my way home.

C: Good, because Xavier and I been standing on the corner forever.

X: Thanks again. I know you hate lying.

C: Yeah. It better have been worth it.
Was it worth it?

X: It was . . . a lot. I have a lot of feelings. But it was fine.

C: ???

X: It just can't last. Something is gonna go wrong.
I'm not allowed to be happy while breaking *all* rules.

C: Maybe you shouldn't break them?

X: Oh, Caridad. I can't wait until you like someone . . .
I'll make sure to send you all these wise-ass texts, too.

C: Girl, bye. With your hotheaded self?
You'll never be wise as me ☺

Sunday, October 28
Braiding

I spent the entire Mass thinking about Aman.
And I can tell Mami is going to lecture me
for not paying any attention.
But thank goodness, as we are leaving church,
Caridad tugs on my hand.

"Señora Batista, is it okay
if Xiomara comes and braids my hair?"
I can tell Mami wants to chew me out
but she can never say no to Caridad.

At her house, Caridad sits between my legs,
and I run the comb through her long thick hair.
I learned to braid when Mami
didn't have time to do mine anymore.

"Two long braids? I can make you look
like Cardi B for Halloween."
I love the reality TV star, but she's everything Caridad isn't.
Caridad gives me a smirk and nods her head.
"Sure. I'll put on old episodes of *Love & Hip Hop*
so you can feel inspired."

Even after I'm done braiding, we sit and watch two more episodes.

Maybe, the only thing that has to make sense
about being somebody's friend
is that you help them be their best self
on any given day. That you give them a home
when they don't want to be in their own.

At least I have a feeling if I asked, that's exactly
what Caridad would say.

Tomorrow is going to be a long-ass day.
But here and now, it's okay.

Monday, October 29
Fights

On Monday afternoon,
I lean against the gate of Twin's genius school.
When Aman asked why I was taking a train downtown
I kissed it off, but I'm sure he'll bring it up later.
So much happened this weekend,
but still I prepared myself for what I knew
I would have to do this afternoon.

Twin gets out an hour later than I do,
and as the kids start filing out after the bell
I spot Twin shuffling my way, but he's not alone.

He's with a tall, red-haired boy,
with fingers the color of milk
that brush lint off my brother's sweater softly
the way Aman sometimes squeezes my hand.

Xavier.

Twin's name never leaves my lips
but somehow he hears me think it.
His head pops in my direction
like a bobble-head doll.

He stumbles back from the white boy so fast
he almost trips on his shoes.
I look between them, confirming what I've always known.
Twin rushes my way and speaks into my ear.

"Xiomara, what are you doing here?"

And I don't need to tell him
I came to knock my knuckles into someone's face.
To redeem his black eye.
To let them know Twin isn't alone.

"You shouldn't have come to my school.
I don't need you to fight for me anymore."

There is a balloon where my heart used to be
and it whooshes air out at the prick of his words.
I look at the boy who gazes at Twin
with love all over his face.

"Leave it alone, Xiomara,"
I think Twin says. But it sounds more like:
"Leave me alone."

Scrapping

I'm not stupid, you know.
I know I'm not gonna be thirty
fighting grown-ass men.
I know I'm not always going to be
bigger and meaner than the boys
in my grade. I know one day,
they'll be stronger and hit back harder.
I know I won't always intimidate girls
with my height, with my hard hands.
I know I won't be able to defend Twin
forever. But I thought when it happened
it would be because he would fight for himself,
not just find *someone else* to protect him.

What We Don't Say

On the train ride home
Twin steps into his feelings
like they're a gated-off room
I don't have visitation rights to.

He spends the entire time
playing chess on his phone.

"Twin. I know you've probably felt this way
your whole entire life but
if Mami and Papi find out about White Boy
they will legit kill you."

His fingers move a rook across the screen,
attacking some imaginary opponent.

"Cody. Not White Boy.
And I know what Mami and Papi will say.
What you're going to say, too."

But *I* don't even know what I'm going to say.
I only know I've always wanted to keep him safe,
but this makes him a target

and I can't defend against the arrows I know are coming.

Gay

I've always known.
Without knowing.
That Twin was.
We never said.
I think he was scared.
I think I was, too.
He's Mami's miracle.
He would become her sin.
I guess I hoped.
If I didn't ever *really* know.
It would be like he wasn't.
But maybe my silence.
Just made him feel more alone.
Maybe my silence.
Condones the ugly things people think.
All that I know.
Is that I don't know
how to move forward
from this.

Feeling Off When Twin Is Mad

A part of myself rebels against the discord.
It might sound dumb, and not all twins are like us,
but when he's angry it throws me off.
I can't think of anything but him being upset
and I'm afraid anything I say will make him angrier.
I don't even know what I did wrong.
I've been fighting dudes for Twin my whole life.
Why did he think I wouldn't show up at his school?
Not even Aman's emoji smiley faces
and links to Ja Rule's old romantic rap videos
are enough to make me feel better.

Rough Draft of Assignment 3—Describe someone you consider misunderstood by society.

When I was little
Mami was my hero.
Because she barely spoke English
and wasn't born here,
but she didn't let that stop her
from defending herself
if she got cut in line at the grocery store,
or from fighting to get Twin into a genius school.
Because I've never seen her
ask my father for money
or complain about her job.
Because her hands will be scraped raw from work
but she still folds them to pray.

When I was little
Mami was my hero.
But then I grew breasts
and although she was always extra hard on me,
her attention became something else,
like she wanted to turn me
into the nun
she could never be.

Final Draft of Assignment 3 (What I Actually Turn In)

Xiomara Batista

Tuesday, November 6

Ms. Galiano

Describe Someone Misunderstood by Society, Final Draft

I've always found Nicki Minaj compelling. Although she gets a bad reputation for being "overly sexual" and making songs like "Anaconda," I think the persona she portrays in her videos is really different from who she is in real life. So, the question should be, "Does society distinguish between who someone actually is and the alter ego they present to the public?" For example, Ms. Minaj may have lyrics that some people feel are a bad influence, but then she's always tweeting people to stay in school.

I also think society puts a negative spin on her music by saying she's allowing men to dictate how she raps, but a lot of her music shows a positive outlook on physical beauty. She is well developed and people always have a lot of negative things to say about her because of her body and how she talks about it and sex, but instead of being ashamed or writing something different, she celebrates her curves and what she wants.

And all that is besides the fact that she also GOT BARS . . . by which I mean to say, she is very artistically talented! She's not just a great "female rapper," she's a great rapper, period.

Ms. Minaj has held her own on tracks with some of the best rappers in the world. She is a woman in a male-dominated world making albums that go platinum. I know she's not considered most women's role model like Eleanor Roosevelt or Mother Teresa, or even Beyoncé, but I think she stands for girls who don't fit into society's cookie-cutter mold. Misunderstood? Perhaps by some. But those of us who can relate, we get her.

At the end of class Ms. Galiano
brings in a student from her poetry club.

He's a Puerto Rican kid I've seen around,
with glasses and a kind smile.

He says his name is Chris,
and he invites us to join the club.

Then he does a short poem
using his hands and his volume to grab our attention.

Ms. Galiano looks on like a proud mama bear,
and the class gives him halfhearted claps, and a dap or two.

Chris hands out flyers for the citywide slam
and personally invites everyone to come to a poetry club meeting.

The slam is three months away.
February 8.

Ms. Galiano says it's open to the public.
And even if we don't sign up

we should attend and support Chris, and our peers.
And I feel my face get hot.

I should be there.
I could compete.

Ice-Skating

When I was little, Mami would take Twin and me
ice-skating every year for our birthday, January 8.
She would work the holidays to make sure
she had the afternoon off. I always think of ice-skating as a gift.

And although Twin is super uncoordinated,
and I've always been a tank in tights,
we were real good at skating.
It was one thing we both did right.

We took to the ice, falling only a few times
before we streamed easily in the circular rink.
Mami would post up behind the glass,
never rented skates herself.
Just watched us turn in circle after circle.
This was a tradition for years.

Until one day it just wasn't.
Until Twin and I stopped asking.
Until I forgot what it felt like to slice through the cold,
maybe like a knife, but mostly like a girl,
skating with her arms out, laughing with her brother
                    while her mother took pictures in the falling snow.

Until

I completely forgot about the skating adventures
we used to go on until Aman asks me to go skating.
I tell him I have to be home straight after school,
and half days won't give us enough time.

"What about tomorrow, no school since teachers are grading
    exams."
And I'm stuck. It *is* a day off
and one when Mami will be at work
so it's not like she'll know I'm not home.

I begin to shake my head,
and then I remember how free I felt on the ice,
how wonderful it was.
And I know I want Aman to see me feeling all that.

Love

Turns out, Aman loves winter sports.
It's the last thing I would have imagined,
but he names professional snowboarders
and skiers, and figure skaters
in the same tone reserved for his favorite rappers.

"X, I'm serious. Even made Pops pay
for a special TV channel so I could keep up."

At first I think he's joking, but the way his eyes light up
I can tell this is really a passion of his.
Maybe like my writing. A secret thing he's loved
that he never felt he could talk about.

He tells me that in Trinidad he was fascinated by snow.
And watching the Winter Olympics was the closest he could get.
And then that became a bigger love.

"X, I'm letting you know right now, I'm nice with the skates.
Prepare to fall in love tomorrow."

And my heart stutters over the word.
How could I do anything but agree to the date?

Thursday, November 8
Around and Around We Go

The next day shines perfect. I invite Twin to come along,
but he only turns his back to me and keeps on pretending to sleep.
He's still upset about my showing up to his school.
And I'm trying to give him space.

Aman is near the skate rental when I arrive,
and all around us kids are walking and laughing.
He holds out a pair of skates and after we're laced up
and have rented a locker we walk awkwardly to the ice.

I take a deep breath at the pang of nostalgia.
So many good memories at Lasker Rink.
I hope to add one more.
I step onto the ice and it all comes back to me.

Aman hasn't moved and I backward skate,
slowly crooking my finger at him.

I blush immediately. I'm never the one to make the first move.
But he seems to like it and steps onto the ice.

He starts off slow. And we both face forward, skating side by side.
Then it's like something comes over him.

And I realize he wasn't lying. He's. Fucking. Amazing.
Aman gets low and gains speed, then does turns and figure eights.
I wait for him to start flipping and somersaulting,
but he just slows down and grabs my hand.

We skate that way for a while, then exit the rink to eat nachos.
"Aman. How did you learn all that? You're so, so good."

He grins at me and shrugs. "I came here and practiced a lot.
My pops never wanted to put me in classes. Said it was too soft."

And now his smile is a little sad.
And I think about all the things we could be
if we were never told our bodies were not built for them.

After Skating

When Aman walks me to the train,
he immediately pulls me to him.
We never kiss so publicly but with his lips on mine
I realize I want the same thing.

And I know that it's stupid,
too easy to run into someone from the block,
or one of Mami's church friends,
but I just want to keep this moment going.

When he tugs on my hand and pulls me even closer,
I let him make me forget:
Twin's anger, confirmation class,
the train smell, the people around us
or the "Stand clear of the closing doors, please."

And I know people are probably staring,
probably thinking: "Horny high school kids
can't keep their hands to themselves."

But I don't care because when our lips meet
for those three stops before I get off,
it's beautiful and real and what I wanted.

We are probably the only thing
worth watching anyways.
Maybe we're doing our train audience a favor.
Reminding them of first love.

This Body on Fire

Walking home from the train
I can't help but think
Aman's made a junkie out of me:

begging for that hit
eyes wide with hunger
blood on fire
licking the flesh
waiting for the refresh
of his mouth.

Fiend begging for an inhale
whatever the price
just so long as
it's real nice.
Real, real nice.
Blood on ice, ice
waiting for that warmth
that heat that fire.

He's turned me into a fiend:
waiting for his next word
hanging on his last breath
always waiting for the next, next time.

The Shit & the Fan

I hear Mami's yelling
through the apartment door
before I even turn the key.

Which isn't right
because she shouldn't be home yet,
it isn't even four o'clock.
I mean, I *did* miss my stop because
I didn't want to quit Aman's kisses.

"Se lo estaba comiendo.
Had her tongue down his throat.
Some little, dirty boy.
I had to get off the train a stop early."

And I know then.
Mami's eyes were a fan
and my make-out session on the train
was the shit hitting it.

Lucky me, she's yelling from her bedroom
and I let myself into the one I share with Twin,
click the door shut, and slide down to put my head
between my legs.

I don't know how much time has passed
before Twin pushes open the door,
and even through the wall of his silence
he understands something is wrong.

He crouches next to me
but I can't warn him of the storm
that's coming.

I can't even be grateful
he's speaking to me again.
I try to make all the big
of me small, small, small.

Miracles

My parents are still yelling in the bedroom,
and because I never yell back at them
I don't scream at my father
when he calls me a cuero.

I don't yell how the whole block whispers
when I walk down the street
about all the women
who made a cuero out of him.

But men are never called cueros.

I don't yell anything
because for the first time in a long time
I'm praying for a miracle.
Pinching myself and hoping
this is all one bad dream.

Trying to unhear
my mother turn my kissing ugly,
my father call me the names
all the kids have called me
since I grew breasts.

God, if you're a thing with ears:
please, please.

Fear

"Xio, what did you do now?"
I don't look at Twin.
Because if I look at him
I'll cry. And if I cry he'll cry.
And if he cries he'll get yelled at
by Papi for crying.

He pushes up to standing
then kneels in front of me again
like his body doesn't know what to do.

"Xio?"

And I want to kick the fear in his voice.

"Xio, do they know you're home yet?
Maybe you can sneak out through
the fire escape? I won't tell. I'll—"

But Mami's chancletas beat
against the floorboards
and Twin and I both know.

He pushes to his feet.
And I see his hands are balled up
into fists he'll never use.
When the footsteps stop outside our door
I stand, brace my shoulders.

"I didn't do anything wrong, Twin.
Go back to your homework.
Or your flirting or whatever."

I didn't do anything at all.

Ants

Mami
    drags
        me
            by
                my
                    shirt

to
    her
        altar
            of
                the
                    Virgin.

Pushes
    me
        down
            until
                I
                    kneel.

"Look the Virgin Mary in the eye, girl. Ask for forgiveness."

I
    bow
        my
            head
                hoping
                    to
                        find
                            air

in
    the
        tiles.
            My
                big
                    is
                        impossible

to
    make
        tiny
            but
                I
                    try

to
    make

ant
of
myself.

"Don't make me get more rice. Mira la Santa María in the eye."

I've
learned
that
ants
hold
ten
times
their
weight—

"Look at her, muchacha, mírala!"

—can
crawl
through
crevices;
have
no
God,
but
crumbs—

"Last chance, Xiomara. 'Santa María, llena eres de gracias . . .'"

—they

    will

        survive

            the

                apocalypse.

Little

    brown

        ants,

          and

            hill-building

          ants,

      and

fire

    ants

          all

  red

       and—

I Am No Ant

My
mother
yanks
my
hair,
pulling
my
face
up
from
the
tiles,
constructing
a
church
arch
of
my
spine
until
Mary's
face
is
an

inch
from
mine;

I
am
no
ant.

Only
sharply
torn.
Something
broken.
In
my
mother's
hand.

Diplomas

"This is why
you want to go
away for college
so you can
open your legs
for any boy
with a big
enough smile.
You think I came
to this country for this?
So you can carry
a diploma
in your belly
but never
a degree?
Tu no vas a ser
un maldito cuero."

Cuero

"Cuero," she calls me to my face.
The Dominican word for *ho*.

This is what a cuero looks like:
A regular girl. Pocket-less jeans
that draw grown men's eyes. Long hair.
A nose ring. A lip ring. A tongue
ring. Extra earrings. Any ring
but a diamond one on her left hand.
Skirts. Shorts. Tank tops. Spaghetti
straps. A cuero lets the world know
she is hot. She can feel the sun.
A spectacular girl. With too much
ass. Too much lip. Too much sass.
Hips that look like water waiting
to be spilled into the hands
of thirsty boys. A plain girl.
With nothing llamativo—nothing
that calls attention. A forgotten girl.
One who parts her hair down the middle.
Who doesn't have cleavage. Whose mouth
doesn't look like it is forever waiting.
Un maldito cuero. I am a cuero, and they're right.
I hope they're right. I am. I am. I AM.

I'll be anything that makes sense
of this panic. I'll loosen myself from this painful flesh.

See, a cuero is any skin. A cuero
is just a covering. A cuero is a loose thing.
Tied down by no one. Fluttering
and waving in the wind. Flying. Flying. Gone.

Mami Says,

"There be no clean in men's hands.
    Even when the dirt has been scrubbed

from beneath nails, when the soap scent
    from them suspends

in the air—there be sins there.
    Their washed hands know how to make a dishrag

of your spine, wring your neck.
    Don't look for pristine handling

when men use your tears for Pine-Sol;
    they'll mop the floor with your pride.

There be no clean there, girl.
    Their fingers were made to scratch dirt,

to find it in the best of things.
    Make your heart a Brillo pad,

brittle and steel—don't be no damn sponge.
    Their fingers don't know to squeeze nicely.

Nightly, if you imagine men's kisses, soft touches, a caress,
    remember Adam was made from clay that stains the hand,

remember that Eve was easily tempted."

Repetition

Mami's hard hands
make me dizzy and nauseous.

Mami prays and prays
while my knees bite into grains of rice.

Mami repeats herself
while her statue of the Virgin watches.

The whole house witnesses
as I pray this steep, steep price.

***Things You Think While You're Kneeling on Rice That Have
Nothing to Do with Repentance:***

I once watched my father peel an orange
without once removing the knife from the fruit.
He just turned and turned and turned it like a globe
being skinned. The orange peel becoming a curl,
the inside exposed and bleeding. How easily he separated
everything that protected the fruit and then passed the bowl
to my mother, dropping that skin to the floor
while the inside burst between her teeth.

Another Thing You Think While You're Kneeling on Rice That Has Nothing to Do with Repentance:

My mother has never had soft hands.
Even when I was a child, they were rough
from pushing wooden mops and scrubbing tiles.

But when I was little I didn't mind.
We would walk down the street
and I would rub her calluses.

She would smile and say
I was her premio for hard work,
I was her premio for patience.

And I loved being her reward.
The golden trophy of her life.
I just don't know when I got too big

for the appointed pedestal.

The Last Thing You Think While You're Kneeling on Rice That Has Nothing to Do with Repentance:

How you will have deep grain-sized indents on your knees.

How lucky you are your jeans protect the skin from breaking.

How you will be walking slow to school.

How kneeling on pews was never as bad as this.

How neither your father nor brother say anything.

How you feel cold but blood has rushed to your face.

How your fists are clenched but they have nothing to hit.

How the stinging pain shoots up your thighs.

How you've never gritted your teeth this tight.

How it hurts less if you force yourself still, still, still.

How pointless these thoughts are. Any of them.

How kissing should never hurt so much.

Leaving

Twin presses a bag
of frozen mixed vegetables
against my knees
and another against my cheek.

"You're lucky, you know.
She's growing old.
She didn't make you kneel very long."

And with the stings
still fresh on my skin
I'm not in a place to nod.
But I know it's true.

"Xio. Just don't get in trouble
until we can leave.
Soon we can leave for college."

I've never heard Twin sound so desperate,
never thought he dreamed of leaving
just like me.

I try not to be resentful he skipped a grade
and will escape sooner.
I try not to be upset at his soft touch.

I elbow him away,
afraid of how my hands
want to hurt everything around me.

What Do You Need from Me?

Is such a simple question.
But when Caridad texts Twin
the message to show to me,
I look at him and hand the phone back.
I'm not mad that he told her.
I know they're both just worried.
But all I need is to give in to
what I wouldn't let myself do in front of Mami:

I curl into a ball and weep.

Consequences

My mother drops the word *no*
like a hundred grains of rice.
I will kneel in these, too.

No cell phone.
No lunch money.
No afternoons off from church.

No boys.
No texting.
No hanging out after school.

No freedom.
No time to myself.
No getting out of confession

with Father Sean this Sunday.

Late That Night

The only person I want
to talk to is Aman.
And although Twin offers
to let me use his phone,
I don't know what I'd say.
That we had a great day,
and that it all fell apart.
That my heart hurts more than my knees.
That we can't be together anymore.
That I would take that beating
again to be with him?
Maybe, there are no words to say.
I just want to be held.

In Front of My Locker

I'm so out of it the next morning
as I put my things away in my locker
that I don't notice the group of guys
circling near until one bumps me,
both his hands palming and squeezing my ass.

And I can tell by how his boys laugh,
how he smirks while saying "oops,"
that this was not an accident.

I scan the hall.
Other kids have slowed down.
Some girls whisper behind their hands.

The group of boys laugh, begin walking away.
Out of the corner of my eye I see Aman
slowing to a standstill. His smile fading.

For the first time since I can remember I wait.
I can't fight today. Everything inside me feels beaten.
And maybe I won't have to.

Aman is here. He'll do something about it.
Of course, as a boy who cares about me,

he's not going to let someone touch me
and make me feel so damn small inside.

Of course, as someone who I've talked to
about how weird it feels to be stared at
and touched like public property,

he'll know how much this bothers me.

But Aman doesn't move.
All the things I needed to tell him about last night,
all the things that have changed since we last kissed on the train
evaporate in the heat of my anger.

I feel my knees throbbing,
the rice bruises pressing into the fabric of my sweats.
And I think about how Aman is the reason
I was punished in the first place.

He's not going to throw a punch.
He's not going to curse or throw a fit.
He's not going to do a damn thing.

Because no one will ever take care of me but me.

Pushing away from my locker,
I face the dude who groped me,

push him hard in the back.
He stumbles but before he can react
I look him dead in the eye:

"If you ever touch me again I'll put my nails
through every pimple on your fucking face."

I push my locker closed and grill Aman before walking away.
"That goes for you, too. Thanks for nothing."

PART |||

The Voice of One

Crying in the Wilderness

Silent World

All of Friday and the weekend
the world I've lived in
wears masking tape
over its mouth.

I wear invisible
Beats headphones
that muffle sound.

I don't hear teachers,
or Father Sean,
Twin, or Caridad.

Aman tries to speak to me
but even in bio
I pretend my ears are cotton filled.

I speak to no one.

The world is almost peaceful
when you stop trying
to understand it.

Sunday, November 11
Heavy

After Mass on Sunday,
under Mami's knowing eyes, I step to Father Sean.
He's kissing babies and talking to old people,
but he gives me his full attention.

I ask to meet him for confession.
And I can't tell if I imagine it,
but his eyes almost seem to get soft.

He glances behind me,
where Mami is standing.

Instead of the confessional, he tells me
to meet him in the rectory,
the well-lit meeting space behind the church.

And I don't know how much truth
my tongue will stumble through.

I walk through the side door and
avoid looking at pictures of the saints.

I'm always avoiding something
and it seems as heavy as any cross.

My Confession

How do you admit a thing like this?
You would think I was pregnant
the way my parents act
like I let them down.

And by my parents, I mean Mami.

Papi mostly huffs around
telling me I better do what Mami says.
And Mami huffs around
saying I better read Proverbs 31 more closely.

And I just want to tell them,
it's NOT THAT DEEP.

I don't got an STD, or a baby.
It was just a tongue. In my mouth.

So I'm not quite sure what to tell
Father Sean when I meet him in the rectory.
Maybe I don't remember my Bible right,
but I don't think this is one of the seven sins.

He sits across from me and crosses his ankles.
"Whenever you're ready we can talk.

I'm guessing you don't need anonymity and I thought
this would be cozier than the confessional. Do you want tea?"

I look at my clasped hands. Because I can't look him in the face.

"I think I committed lust. And disobeyed my parents . . .
although they never actually said I couldn't kiss a boy
on the train, so I'm not sure if that's the right sin."

I wait for Father Sean to speak,
but he just stares at the picture of the pope above me.
"Are you actually sorry, Xiomara?"
I wait a moment. Then I shake my head, no. Say:

"I'm sorry I got in trouble.
I'm sorry I have to be here.
That I have to pretend to you and her
that I care about confirmation at all.
But I'm not sorry I kissed a boy.
I'm only sorry I was caught.
Or that I had to hide it at all."

Father Sean Says,

"Our God is a forgiving God.
Even when we do things we shouldn't
our God understands the weakness of the flesh.
But forgiveness is only granted
if the person is actually remorseful.
I think this goes much deeper
than kissing a boy on the train."

Prayers

Father Sean is Jamaican.
His Spanish has a funky accent
and when he gives the gospel for the Latino Mass
half of the words be sounding made up.

It makes the younger kids laugh;
it makes our older folks smile.

His Spanish, when he talks to my mother,
does neither. His hazel eyes are sure
and gentle when he looks at Mami
and tells her:

"Altagracia, I don't think Xiomara
is quite ready to be confirmed.
I think she has some questions
we should let her answer first."

He explains it's not what I confessed.
But several questions I've asked
and comments I've made
make him think I should keep
coming to classes if I'd like
but not take the leap of confirmation this year.

My mother's face scrunches tight
like someone has vacuumed all her joy.

I avoid her eyes
but something must flash in them
because Father Sean raises a hand.

"Altagracia, please be calm.
Remember anger is as much a sin
as any Xiomara may have committed.
We all need time to come to terms
with certain things, don't we?"

And I don't know
if Father Sean just granted me a blessing
or nailed my coffin shut.

How I Can Tell

I can tell when Mami is really angry
because her Spanish becomes faster than usual.
The words bumping into one another like go-karts.

"Mira, muchacha . . . You will not embarrass me in church again.
From now on, you're going to fix yourself.
Do you hear me, Xiomara?

No te lo voy a decir otra vez."
(But I know she *will* in fact tell me again. And again.)
"There are going to be some big changes."

Before We Walk in the House

"You cannot turn your back on God.
I was on my journey to the convent,
prepared to be his bride,
when I married your father.

I think it was punishment.
God allowed me America
but shackled me with a man addicted to women.

It was punishment,
to withhold children from me for so long
until I questioned if anyone in this world would ever love me.

But even business deals are promises.
And we still married in a church.
And so I never walked away from him

although I tried my best to get back
to my first love.
And confirmation is the last step I can give you.

But the child sins just like the parent.
Because look at you, choosing this over the sacred.
I don't know if you're more like your father

or more like me."

231

My Heart Is a Hand

That tightens
into a fist.
It is a shrinking thing,
like a raisin,
like a too-tight tee,
like fingers that curl
but have no other hand
to hold them
so they just end up
biting into themselves.

Wednesday, November 14
A Poem Mami Will Never Read

Mi boca no puede escribir una bandera blanca,
nunca será un verso de la Biblia.
Mi boca no puede formarse el lamento
que tú dices tú y Dios merecen.

Tú dices que todo esto
es culpa de mi boca.
Porque tenía hambre,
porque era callada.
pero ¿y la boca tuya?

Cómo tus labios son grapas
que me perforan rápido y fuerte.

Y las palabras que nunca dije
quedan mejor muertas en mi lengua
porque solamente hubieran chocado
contra la puerta cerrada de tu espalda.

Tu silencio amuebla una casa oscura.
Pero aun a riesgo de quemarse,
la mariposa nocturna siempre busca la luz.

In Translation

My mouth cannot write you a white flag,
it will never be a Bible verse.
My mouth cannot be shaped into the apology
you say both you and God deserve.

And you want to make it seem
it's my mouth's entire fault.
Because it was hungry,
and silent, but what about your mouth?

How your lips are staples
that pierce me quick and hard.

And the words I never say
are better left on my tongue
since they would only have slammed
against the closed door of your back.

Your silence furnishes a dark house.
But even at the risk of burning,
the moth always seeks the light.

Heartbreak

I never meant to hurt anyone.
I didn't see how I could
by stealing kisses
as I whispered promises into ears
that I know now weren't listening.
I pretend not to see him in the hallway.
I pretend not to see them at home.
The ultimate actress because I'm always pretending,
pretending I'm blind, pretending I'm fine;
I should win an Oscar I do it so well.

Is this remorse? Is this worthy of forgiveness?

Reminders

I lie in bed doing homework
while Twin watches anime on YouTube.

He's stopped wearing his headphones,
so that I can listen in.

(It's technically breaking Mami's rules,
but she would never punish Twin.)

Halfway through an episode a commercial
endorsed by one of last year's Winter Olympians comes on.

And I must make a noise,
because Twin looks over his shoulder at me.

He quiets his laptop. "Are you okay?"

But I just bury my head in my pillow.
And remind myself to breathe.

Writing

The next day and the one after that,
I spend every class writing in my journal.
Ms. Galiano sends me to the guidance counselor
but I refuse to talk to her either
until she threatens to call home,
so I make up an excuse about cramps and stress.

Hiding in my journal
is the only way I know not to cry.
My house is a tomb.
Even Twin has stopped speaking to me
as if he's afraid a single word
will cause my facade to crack.

I hear Mami on the phone
making plans to send me to D.R. for the summer;
the ultimate consequence:
let that good ol' island living fix me.

Every time I think about being away from home,
from English, from Twin and Caridad, I feel like a ship at sea:
all the possibilities to end up anywhere I want,
all the possibilities to be lost.

What I'd Like to Tell Aman When He Sends Another Apology Message:

Your hands on mine were cold
Your lips near my ear were warm
Your "I'm sorry" fervent
But you have no need to apologize
I know silence well
None of this was ever about you
You were just a failed rebellion
(Of course   I'm lying
You were everything
But I can't have you
Without entering a fight I won't win)
I know none of these were battles
That I wanted in the first place

Favors

The night before Thanksgiving,
Twin pulls my headphones out,
offers me a sliced-up apple
and a soft smile.

"You haven't been eating much."

I take the plate and stare at the fruit,
surprised he's even noticed.

"I'm just not hungry."
I eat everything but the seeds.
Because I know that Twin is worried.
And I really can't resist apples.

"Xiomara, can I ask you a favor?
Will you write a poem about love?
One about being thankful
that a person is in your life?"

I look at my brother blankly.
I wonder if he knows
how close he is

to having his face pierced
by apple seeds.

Something in my gut
rebels against the apple
and I feel it wanting to come
all the way back up my throat.

For a second I think of all the poems
that I wrote for Aman,
but I push the thought away.

I shove the plate at Twin.
"You want me to write a love poem
for your . . . for White Boy?
Was that what this apple was all about?"

Twin stares at me, baffled,
and then something clears on his face.
He pulls my empty plate against his chest, like armor.
"His name is Cody.
And the poem was actually for you.
I thought it would be cathartic
to write something beautiful for yourself."

Pulled Back

I'm helping Mami dice potatoes and beets
for her ensalada rusa when the phone rings.

She answers and passes it to me.
And I can't imagine who it is.
Caridad's voice screeches in my ear:

"Listen, woman, I know you're upset.
I know you got a lot going on.
But don't you dare ignore me for two weeks straight.
Just because you got your cell taken you can't call nobody?"

And instead of getting angry, I actually tear up.
It's such a small thing. But also *so* normal.
Caridad never takes my shit
and she lets me know this time is no different.

She sighs and her voice softens.
"I'm worried about you, Xio. Don't shut us out."

And she can't see me nodding through the phone.
But I murmur an apology. And tell her I have to go.
And I know she knows I'm really saying "thank you."

Thursday, November 22
On Thanksgiving

El Día de Acción de Gracias,
Twin and I join Mami at church
and help spoon mashed potatoes
and peas and other American things
we never eat at home
onto homeless people's plates.
I feel sick the whole day.
Like everyone can see
that the only thing I'm thankful for
is Mami's silence.
Even Twin, who looks at me
with his puppy dog face,
makes me want to overturn the table,
and crush all these mushy peas beneath my heel.

Haiku: The Best Part About Thanksgiving Was When Mami:

Returned my cell.
Until I remember I've
got no one to text.

Rough Draft of Assignment 4–When was the last time you felt free?

I must have been five or six,
because the memory is fuzzy.

But my father had been watching
a karate movie on TV,

and my mother was at church,
so there was no one to bother us.

Twin and I tied long-sleeved T-shirts
around our heads

and used the bows from my church dresses
to tie like karate sashes around our waists.

We thought this made us look like ninjas
and we hopped from couch to couch,

sliding off the plastic sofa covers
but never landing in the "lava."

(Why were we ninjas in volcanoes? Who knows.)

I remember at one point looking up
and seeing my mother in the living room doorway—

I flung myself at her. There was freedom there,
in flying. In believing I'd be caught.

I can't remember if she did catch me.
But she must have, or wouldn't I remember falling?

Rough Draft of Assignment 4–When was the last time you felt free?

Maybe the last time I was happy saying a poem?
With Aman listening to me, eyes half closed—
that moment right before I opened my mouth,
when I was nervous and my heart thumped fast,
but I knew I could do it anyway, that I could
say something, anything, in this moment
and someone was going to listen.

Rough Draft of Assignment 4—When was the last time you felt free?

Can a stoop be a place of freedom?
I feel like any time I sat on a stoop
I could just watch the world
without it watching me too closely.
Over the summer, it feels like years ago,
the downstairs stoop was a playground.
It was a moment when I could breathe
without anyone asking me to do or be
anything other than what I was:
a girl, an almost woman, sitting
in the sunshine and enjoying the warmth.
Dudes don't bother you too much
when you're sitting on your own apartment stoop.
When I sat on the stoop with the boy
I thought really cared for me there was freedom then, too.
In the ways our bodies leaned toward each other,
in the fact that I finally let myself be reckless.
There is freedom in coming and going
for no other reason than because you can.
There is freedom in choosing to sit and be still
when everything is always telling you to move, move fast.

Final Draft of Assignment 4 (What I Actually Turn In)

Xiomara Batista

Tuesday, December 4

Ms. Galiano

Last Time You Felt Free, Final Draft

Freedom is a complicated word. I've never been imprisoned like Nelson Mandela or some people I grew up with. I've never been encaged like a Rottweiler used for dogfights, or like the roosters my parents grew up tending. Freedom seems like such a big word. Something too big; maybe like a skyscraper I've glimpsed from the foot of the building but never been invited to climb.

Gone

Even lunch
has now become
another place
I absolutely hate.
A group of boys
has started stopping
by our quiet table
trying to squeeze in
next to us
or look at what
the girls are drawing.
Or trying to sneak peeks
at my notebook.
These are boys
from some of my classes,
some even smoke with Aman.
Sometimes the teacher
on duty notices.
If it's Ms. Galiano, I'm safe.
If it's not, I have to hope
it's another teacher
who gives a damn
about the quiet girls
in the corner.

I can't afford
any more trouble.
So I keep my hands
in my lap.
I keep my mouth
zippered shut.
And every day
I wish I could
just become
a disappearing act.

Monday, December 10
Zeros

When Ms. Galiano returns Assignment 4
I'm expecting a red zero by my name.
But instead, there's a note:

Xiomara,

*Is everything okay? Let's talk after class. I've noticed your
workmanship seems less thoughtful than usual and you
failed another quiz. See me.*

I try to think of the ways
I can sneak out unnoticed.
I have nothing to say
to Ms. Galiano, or anyone else.

I fold the assignment sheet
into small, small squares
until I can squeeze it like a fortune
tightly held in the center of my palm.

Possibilities

Ms. Galiano is sneaky.
Before the bell rings
she calls me to her desk
and asks me to stand with her
while she dismisses the other students,

and she doesn't even try to ease
into the conversation neither:

"What's going on?
You aren't submitting assignments,
and you're even quieter than usual."

But I don't have anything to tell her.
If nothing else, my family believes
in keeping las cosas de la casa en la casa—
what happens in house, stays in house.

So I just shrug.

"What about poetry club?
I keep expecting you to show up.
Your writing is so good.
You wouldn't even have to read.
Maybe you just come and listen, see how you feel?"

I almost tell her I have a confirmation class,
that the times overlap.

But then I remember, Father Sean
isn't expecting me to show up anymore . . .
and well, Mami is. Who would know I'm skipping
as long as I'm there when she picks me up?

Plus, I have so much bursting to be said,
and I think I'm ready to be listened to.
I swallow back the smile that tries to creep
onto my face but tell Ms. Galiano:

"I'll redo the assignment, if I can.
And I'll see you at the club tomorrow."

Can't Tell Me Nothing

I don't know the last time I looked forward to something.
The afternoons with Aman seem so long ago.
We're in a new unit now and Mr. Bildner
has changed our lab partners.
I'm with a girl named Marcy who doodles hearts
over and over in her notebook.

Sometimes I catch Aman looking at me from across the room.
Long looks that stretch the physical space between us,
and although I'm still angry that he didn't stand up for me
a part of me feels like maybe I messed up, too.

But even if I wanted to fix it, there's really no reason why.
He and I can't have anything to do with each other.
Looking back, maybe we had a parasitic relationship?
One of us taking and the other only trying to stay afloat.

Maybe it's better we ended. Because what can I give him?
Nothing but infrequent kisses. Nothing but half-done poems.
Nothing but sneaking around and regret at all my lying.
Nothing. But at least there's tomorrow. At least there's poetry.

Tuesday, December 11
Isabelle

"Ain't you the big-body freshman
all the boys always talking about?"

I look at the only other person
in Ms. Galiano's room,

a girl in a pink tutu and Jordans
who must be some kind of mixed.

Despite my sweaty hands and racing heart
I almost laugh.

I don't know why I thought poetry club
would be any different than the rest of the world.

I shrug. "I'm actually a sophomore."

She cocks her head at me, and pats the seat next to her.
"I'm Isabelle, who woulda thought you was a poet? Dope."

First Poetry Club Meeting

It's funny how the smallest moments
are like dominoes lining up,
being stacked with the purpose
of knocking you on your ass.
In a good way.

I should be tight over Isabelle's comment;
instead, I like how straight-up she is.
Most people talk about me behind my back,
but she says whatever is on her mind.

I don't want to get excited,
because who knows if I'll even come back,
but it seems Ms. Galiano's small stack of posters
called a cute little mix of people.

We are four in total, a small club,
two boys—Chris, who did a poem in my class
before handing out flyers, and Stephan,
who's *super* quiet. Then Isabelle from the Bronx.

Ms. Galiano welcomes me to the club
and asks everyone to read a poem
as a way for them
to introduce themselves to me.

Chris and Isabelle have theirs memorized,
but Stephan reads from his notebook.
My hands are shaking even before
it's my turn and I just keep hoping
somehow I'll be skipped.

Stephan's poetry is filled with the most colorful images.
Each line a fired visual, landing on target.
(I don't always understand every line
but love the pictures being painted behind my eyelids.)

Chris Hodges is loud, a mile-a-minute talker,
a comment for every poem, everything is "Deep" and "Wow,"
his own poem using words like *abyss* and *effervescent*
(I think he's studying for the SAT).

And then there's Isabelle Pedemonte-Riley.
Her piece rhymes and she sounds
like a straight-up rapper. You can tell she loves
Nicki Minaj, too. That girl's a storyteller
writing a world you're invited to walk into.

I sit wondering how writing can bring
such strange strangers into the same room.

And then it's my turn to read.

Nerves

I open my mouth but can't push the words out.
It's not like when I read to Aman.
Although I wanted him to like it,
I didn't feel like I had to impress him.

But right now I'm nervous
and the poem doesn't feel done yet,
or like a poem at all, just a journal entry.

A fist tightens in my stomach
and I take a breath trying to unclench it.

I've never imagined an audience for my work.
If anything my poems were meant to be seen and not heard.

The room is so quiet, and I clear my throat—
even my pause sounds too loud.
Isabelle speaks up.

"You got this, girl. Just let us hear every word."

Ms. Galiano nods,
and Stephan gives a soft "mhmm."
And so I grip my notebook tight and launch into the piece.

When I'm Done

Isabelle snaps, and Ms. Galiano smiles,
and of course, Chris has a comment
about my poem's complex narrative structure,
or something like that.

I can't remember
the last time people were silent
while I spoke, actually listening.

Not since Aman.
But it's nice to know I don't need him
in order to feel listened to.

My little words
feel important, for just a moment.
This is a feeling I could get addicted to.

Compliments

"You did a great job today, Xiomara.
I know it isn't always easy
to put yourself out there like that," Ms. Galiano says.

And although I'm used to compliments
they're rarely ever about my thoughts,
so I can't stop the smile that springs onto my face.
I make sure to swallow it before it blooms too big.

But it feels like an adult has finally really heard me.
And for the first time since the "incident"
I feel something close to happiness.

And I want to stay and talk to the other kids,
or to Ms. Galiano, but when I look up at the clock
I know I have to rush to church or Mami will know
that I skipped out. So instead, I just say "Thank you"
and leave without looking back.

Caridad Is Standing Outside the Church

C: Confirmation let out early.
Your mother's inside saying a prayer.
I told her you were using the bathroom.

X: Shit. I'm sorry. I know you hate lying to her.

C: It's okay, Xiomara. But listen,
you were mad lucky
Father Sean went straight
to the rectory after class.

X: I know, I know.
He would have blown up my whole spot.

C: Are you dealing with that boy again?

X: Actually, I was with two boys. And a girl.
Oh my God, you look like you might pass out!
I was at a poetry club meeting. There were other kids there. Relax.

C: You almost gave me a heart attack.
Speaking of poetry, I heard about an open mic
happening this Friday. We haven't had a social activity in a while.
Down to go with me?

X: I can't go, Caridad.
You know Mami won't let me.
I'm still in trouble.

C: She'll let you go
as long as it's with me and Xavier.

Hope Is a Thing with Wings

Although I doubt it,
hope flies quick into
my body's corners.

Thursday, December 13
Here

Although Mami still huffs
like a dragon at home
and Aman has stopped
trying to say I'm sorry
and Twin seems sadder
and sadder every day
and my silence feels like a leash
being yanked in all directions
I actually raise my hand
in English class
and answer Ms. Galiano's question.
Because at least here with her,
I know my words are okay.

Haikus

Cafeterias
do not seem like safe places.
Better to chill, hide.

*

I skipped the lunchroom.
Instead I sit, write haikus
inside bathroom stalls.

*

Haikus are poems.
They have three lines, follow rules
of five-seven-five.

*

Traditionally
contrasting ideas are
tied together neat.

*

I'm like a haiku,
with different sides,
except no clean tie.

*

I count syllables,
using my fingers to help
until the bell rings.

Offering

I gather my thoughts and things
when the bathroom door flings open.
Head down, I begin rushing out
when I hear the high-pitched voice:

"Hey, X."

I look up to see Isabelle,
in a denim shirt and another frilly-ass skirt,
her curly blond fro
with a mind of its own frames her stare.

"Tell me you ain't eat lunch in the bathroom?"

I clear my half-eaten lunch off the tray
and into the trash. Without a word reach for the door.

"Just because I saw you at poetry club
doesn't mean we're homies"
is what I *don't* say but want to.

Isabelle puts a gentle hand on my shoulder;
that hand stops me in my tracks.

"X, I go into the photography room during lunch,
to eat and work on writing.
It's quiet on this end of the floor
and the art teacher lets me chill.
Come through if you'd like."

Holding Twin

I click the front door closed
and reach for the house phone
to call Mami so she knows I'm in on time,
but I feel Twin's loud sob shake me to my bones.

I drop my bag at the door
and rush to the bedroom,
where Twin is curled
on my bed, crying
into a stuffed elephant.

And for once,
I'm glad we don't need words.
I brush his curls and sit beside him.

And I know something has happened
with the red-haired boy.

"Did you get in another fight?"
I ask, and shake him hard.
"Was it Cody? Was he the one that hit you before?"

But even through his tears
Twin looks at me like I'm crazy.

"No, he didn't hit me. Cody would never.
That black eye was just some idiot in gym.
This, this is so much worse."

Cody

Twin's story comes out in pieces:
He met Cody's family last week,
when his parents dropped him off at school.
Apparently they loved Twin (who wouldn't)
and wanted him to come over for dinner.

(Parents being accepting of sexuality
seems all kinds of bizarre to me
because the thought of what my parents would do
if they knew makes every bone in my body hurt.)

It seemed perfect, Twin says,
finally a person and place and family
that accept him for who he is.

But it turns out Cody's father
is being relocated for his job
after winter break and Cody
thinks long distance will be too hard.

So he broke it off with Twin.
And seems to have cracked
something inside him in the process.

I hold Twin close to me,
and rock him back and forth.

"Us Batista twins have no luck with love.
You would have thought we'd be smarter
guarding our hearts."

Problems

Twin can't stop shaking,
his whole skinny body trembling,
and he's breathing so hard
his glasses keep fogging up.

I take them off his face and pat his back,
tell him we'll figure this out together.
That with a bit more time and space
it'll all feel clearer.

I glance at the clock.
"You need to calm down a bit;
Mami will be home soon . . . Shit."

Mami! I forgot to call her.

Dominican Spanish Lesson:

Brava (feminine ending), adj. meaning fierce, ferocious, mad tempered.

As in: Mami was mad brava when she came home because I hadn't called her. And even more so when she saw Twin crying and thought I had done something to him.

As in: I became brava Twin didn't correct her. (I think he was too busy biting back sobs. And the last thing I'm going to do right now is correct Mami on anything.)

As in: We're both brava; she's already threatening to send me to D.R. after winter break instead of during the summer. (The last thing I need to do is get on her bad side.)

As in: She was so brava her whole face shook and she began praying underneath her breath then she just pointed to the bathroom and I knew she meant for me to clean it.

Permission

When Caridad calls later that night
Mami listens to her talk on the phone.
And although Mami sounds all nice
she keeps shooting me the shadiest looks.

Finally, she says, "Está bien." Fine.
I can go with Caridad to a poetry event.
But only if Twin comes along, too.

I am sure convincing him will be tough.
His eyes are so swollen from crying
he's had to lie to my parents and tell them
he rubbed his eyes after a chemistry lab gone wrong.

But when I mention the open mic night
he must want any excuse not to think of Cody
because he quickly agrees to come along.

Friday, December 14
Open Mic Night

The legendary Nuyorican Poets Cafe
is not close to Harlem.

It takes us two trains and a walk in the
brick-ass cold to get there, and when we do,
the line to get in is halfway down the block.

Not even nightclubs around the way
look half as packed as this.

The cafe is dimly lit, with paintings on the wall.
The host is a statuesque black woman
with a bright red flower in her hair.

When she calls out the names on her list,
I'm surprised to hear my own.

Signed Up

Caridad tells me she signed me up to perform
and immediately my hands start shaking.
I've got to get out of here right-right now.
But Caridad is having none of it.
She just grabs my arm and Twin pulls me
along with the other.

"You got this, Xio."

But every time someone gets onstage
I compare myself to them.
Is my poem going to make
people say *mmmm* or snap?
What if nobody claps?

Some of the poets are so, so good.
They make the audience laugh,
they make me almost cry,
they use their bodies and faces
and know just how to talk into the mic.

The host keeps the show moving
and as another person gets offstage I know
my name is creeping up her list until

her clear, crisp voice calls out, "Xiomara."
And I'm frozen stiff.

"I think she's shy, y'all.
Someone told me she's an open mic newbie.
Keep clapping, keep clapping, keep clapping
until she gets to the stage."

And so now not only am I frozen stiff,
I'm also blushing and breaking into a sweat.
But somehow, I'm on my feet
and then the lights bright on my face
make me double blink hard and the cafe
that seemed so small before feels like it has
a Madison Square Garden–sized audience now.

I have never experienced a silence like this.
A hundred people waiting.
Waiting for me to speak.

And I don't think I can do it.
My hands are shaking too much,
and I can't remember the first line of the poem.
Just a big-ass blank yawning in my memory.
My heart dribbles hard in my chest
and I look at the nearest exit,
at the stairs leading to the stage—

The Mic Is Open

—and the first line clicks.
I say it, my voice trembling.
I clear my throat.
I take a breath.
I begin the poem all over again.
I forget the comparisons.
I forget the nerves.
I let the words fill the room.
I let the words carry me away.

People watch. They listen,
and when I'm done
saying a poem I've practiced
in my mirror, they clap.
And it sounds so loud
that I want to cover my ears,
cover my face. Two poets
perform after me but I don't hear
a word with my heart in my ears.
Caridad squeezes my hand,
and Twin, looking happy for a moment,
whispers, "You killed that shit."

But it's not until we're leaving
when the host grabs me by the arm

and says, "You did that.

You should come to this youth slam

I'm hosting in February.

I think it'd be really powerful."

That's when I know,

I can't wait to do this again.

Invitation

The slam the host tells me about
is the same one that Ms. Galiano
has mentioned at poetry club.
And I'm not the type to believe
"everything is a sign" or whatever,
but when so many parts of my life
all point in one direction . . .
it's hard not to follow the arrows.

Even when I'm home,
my hands are still shaking.
And I try not to appear
as overwhelmed as I feel.

For the first time in a long time,
Twin doesn't look sad or distracted.
He just keeps turning to me in our room,
his face glowing. "Xiomara. That. Was. Amazing."

Although I've never been drunk or high
I think it must feel like this:
off balance, giggly, unreal.

I know exactly what Twin means.

Because so many of the poems tonight
felt a little like our own stories.
Like we saw and were seen.
And how crazy would it be
if I did that for someone else?

Sunday, December 16
All the Way Hype

The whole weekend I relive the open mic.
Saturday and Sunday I have to bite back my excitement.
I write between cleaning.
I write instead of doing homework.
I write before *and* after church on Sunday.
I can't wait for poetry club.
Going there was like being tested in fire;
it helped me to be brave,
so I can't wait to tell them about the Nuyo.

Late into the night I write and
the pages of my notebook swell
from all the words I've pressed onto them.
It almost feels like
the more I bruise the page
the quicker something inside me heals.

Tuesday has become my equivalent
to Mami's Sunday. A prayer circle.

Monday, December 17
At Lunch on Monday

I go to the art room
and Isabelle is there with headphones
and a journal and a bag of spicy Doritos.
I sit across the long table from her
and open my notebook.

Suddenly she looks up and slides
the huge headphones off.
"Tell me what you think."

She starts reading,
her hands fluttering in the air.
I put my apple down to focus,
because this feels like an important moment.

When she's done, she doesn't look at me.
And Isabelle isn't the type *not* to look at someone.
I don't tell her it's good, even though it is.
I don't tell her it's beautiful, although it's that, too.

"That gave me chills," I say.
"I felt it here," I say.
"You should finish it," I say.

And when she smiles at me
I smile back.

Tuesday, December 18
At Poetry Club

I let everyone know I went to an open mic.

They seem amazed.
Ask me for details.

Tell me they want to go along
the next time I perform.

And I feel such a rush
at the way Isabelle grabs my hand and squeals.

The way Ms. Galiano smiles
like I did something to make her proud.

"How did you do?" Chris asks.
I shrug. "I didn't suck."

And everyone smiles,
because they know that means I killed it.

Every Day after English Class

Ms. Galiano asks me to read her something new.
With five minutes between classes,
I know I need to pick the best and shortest pieces in advance.
But every day I pick a new poem and I have learned:
to slow down, to breathe, to pace myself, to show emotion.

The last day before winter break
Ms. Galiano tells me I'm really blossoming.

And I think about what it means
to be a closed bud, to become open.
And even though it's cliché, it's also perfect.

When I see Stephan in the hallway,
he reads me his latest haiku.
When I see Chris on my way to the train,
he always has a smile for me
and a "Wassup, X! Write anything new?"

And I know that I'm ready to slam.
That my poetry has become something I'm proud of.
The way the words say what I mean,
how they twist and turn language,
how they connect with people.
How they build community.

I finally know that all of those
"I'll never, ever, ever"
stemmed from being afraid but not even they
can stop me. Not anymore.

Christmas Eve

My mother doesn't buy a Christmas tree.
Instead she buys three big poinsettias
and sets them on a red tablecloth
on the living room windowsill.

Noche Buena, the Good Night,
has always been one of my favorite holidays.
On TV white families
always open gifts on Christmas Day,
but most Latinos celebrate the night before.

During the day Caridad comes over,
bringing her mother's famous coquito
that's laced with a little bit of rum.
We play video games with Twin
and exchange cards we made for each other.

Mami has always made Twin and me
go to the Midnight Mass to celebrate Baby Jesus
and when we get back we've been allowed to open gifts.

This year when we get home from church
I go straight to my room.

I know better than to expect anything.

I lie in bed, with Chance the Rapper in my ear,
when there's a knock on the door.
I look, imagining it's Twin trying to be respectful.
Except it's not. Mami stands there.
With a small wrapped box in her hand.

She shuffles into the room, sets the gift on the desk,
and like she doesn't know what to do with her hands
she picks up Twin's sweater from the computer chair
and neatly refolds it.
When she sits, I sit up in bed, unsure of what to do.

But just as fast as she sits down she stands,
gestures to the gift, and walks to the door.
"I had it resized for you.
I know how much you like jewelry."

It's a Rosary

I think before I open the box.
My mother doesn't believe
in any other kind of jewelry.

But when I lift the lid,
I see a small gold plaque
with my name etched on it,
a thin gold chain making
the bracelet complete.

And I know I've seen
this plaque before.
When I turn it over
I remember where.
Inscribed on the inside
are two Spanish words:
Mi Hija.

This was my baby bracelet.
Mami must have kept it
all these years.
But why she resized it now
makes absolutely no sense.

I lay it across my wrist
and cinch the clasps closed.
Her daughter on one side,
myself on the other.

And I feel so many things
but mostly relief that it wasn't a rosary.

Wednesday, December 26–Tuesday, January 1
Longest Week

The week after Christmas is the longest week of my life.
I write and I write and I read poems to Twin,
who is still in his feelings and refusing
to talk to me about Cody, but I see him texting Caridad,
who's the most sympathetic of us all,
so probably a good decision.

I read the poems so often and edit so much
that I begin memorizing them by accident
until my head is full of words and stories,
until I'm practicing the poems in my dreams.
And the more I write the braver I become.

I write about Mami, about feeling like an ant,
about boys trying to always holler at me,
about Aman, about Twin. Sometimes I'm still awake
writing when Mami gets up at the ass crack of dawn
to go to work. So many words fill my notebook
and I can't wait to share them all.

But still another week to go until poetry club.

Wednesday, January 2
The Waiting Game

Because of New Year's,
we don't start school again until Wednesday.

So I miss poetry club by just one day.

Although I'm disappointed,
the extra week gives me more time to write.

Isabelle and I share some poems during lunch.

And if I catch Stephan or Chris in the hallways,
we'll joke or talk about a new piece.

With my birthday in a week,
I realize that this new year hasn't started off so bad.

Tuesday, January 8
Birthdays

On our birthday Twin and I exchange gifts in the morning
right before we leave for school.

I got him an X-Men comic, issue 17.
Although it's not his usual anime,

Twin tears up when he sees it.
Iceman, the main character in it,

is a super-dope gay mutant.
I hug him awkwardly, and before he pulls away:

"I don't know if I told you.
But I'm on your side. Always."

Twin gives me a tight hug
and hands me a wrapped package.

I break open the tape and see the leather cover.
It's another notebook, so similar to my first.

"Ran out of gift ideas?" I tease.

He shakes his head and nods at my old notebook,
fat and falling apart on the kitchen table.

"No, and your old one is so full I know you haven't either."

We pack up and walk arm in arm to the train.
Today will be a good day.

The Good

Caridad has left me five voice mails singing "Happy Birthday."
They're ridiculous and her voice is horrible,
but I laugh every time. I'm sure she's trying to get up
to sixteen by the end of the day.

When I go put away my bio textbook before lunch,
an envelope flutters to the ground.
Inside I find a printed-out receipt for two admission tickets
to an apple farm just north of the Bronx.

Only one person at this school knows
how much I love apples. Aman.
A laugh uncurls in my throat and stretches its way to my lips.

By the time poetry club comes around,
I'm walking on air before Stephan pulls me into the classroom,
Chris takes off his fitted and croons "Happy Birthday"—
the Stevie Wonder version.

Isabelle hands me a cupcake.
Ms. Galiano gives me a wink.
I think I will remember this birthday for the rest of my life.

The Bad

When we start going around the room
to read our poems I reach into my bag.

I find the new journal Twin gave me,
but after searching and searching, I realize

I must have left my old one on the kitchen table.

For a moment I feel so anxious:
all those poems I wrote over break,
and I don't even have one to share.

But I try from memory;
one of my favorites
rolls off my tongue
as if I planned it that way.

It feels so good to do a new poem.
And so good to listen
to Chris, Stephan, and Isabelle.

And when I finally look at the clock
I realize I'm running late to church.

At some point Mami will find out
I haven't been going to confirmation classes.
Probably when the class is confirmed
and I don't have an excuse for poetry club anymore.

But for now, I'm going to keep frontin'.
I just need to get to church before she's waiting outside.

I grab my bag in a hurry,
leave with a quick wave, not my usual good-bye,
and zip my North Face up tight.

I grab my phone to shoot Caridad a text
and see I have two missed calls.

My mother's voice mail
spears ice into my bones:

"Te estoy esperando en casa."

Click.

The Ugly

I'm breathing hard by the time I get home.
I ran from the train and my face is flushed.

I glance at the kitchen table before hurrying
to my room—my notebook isn't there.

Mami is sitting on the edge of my bed
with my journal cradled between her hands.

When she looks at me,
I feel blood rush from my cheeks.

I hear a baseball game in the living room,
but I know neither Papi nor Twin can save me.

My hands pulse to grab the book from her
but I don't move from the doorway.

She speaks softly: "You think I don't know
enough English to figure out you talk about boys

and church and me? To know all these terrible things you think?"

My mother has always seemed like a big woman
even though she's so much smaller than I am.

This moment when she swells up and stands
I shrink in the eyes of her wrath.

"These thoughts you have, that you would write them,
for the people to read . . . without feeling guilt. Shame.

What kind of daughter of mine *are* you?"

She seems lost. As if I've yanked an anchor
from the only thing that's kept her afloat.

She grabs the book in one hand
and it's then that I notice the box of matches.

The box that's always on the stove.
The one that's sitting on my bed.

I don't know what an asthma attack feels like.
But it has to be like this:

like claws reaching into your chest
and snatching sharply every bit of air—leaving you breathless

and wounded before you know what's happened—

she's lit the match.

Let Me Explain

I tell her.
That no one sees the words.
      That they're just my personal thoughts.
That it helps for me to write them down.
      That they're private.
That she wasn't supposed to ever read my poems.

That I'm sorry.
      That I'm sorry.
            That I'm sorry.

And I'm digging my fingers into the doorframe.
    It's the only thing holding me up,

                        holding me back.

My anger wants to become a creature
      with teeth and nails but I keep it collared
because this is my mother. And I *am* sorry.

That she found it,   that I wrote it,   that I ever thought
      my thoughts were mine.

She holds the lit match up
                to a corner of my notebook.

"Get a trash can, Xiomara.
I don't want ashes on my floor."

If Your Hand Causes You to Sin

"If your hand causes you to sin . . .
If your eye causes you to sin . . .
If this notebook, this writing, causes you to sin . . ."

The smell of burning leather propels me.
I push from the doorway
and reach for her hand.
Hundreds of poems, I think.
Years and years of writing.

She turns before I can get my hand on the notebook,
shoves her elbow hard into my chest.
Recites the words loud again and again.

"If your hand causes you to sin . . .
If your eye causes you to sin . . .
If this notebook, this writing, causes you to sin . . ."

And for the first time in my life
I understand the word *desperate*.
How it's a pointed hunger in the belly.

Please. Please. Please.

She holds me off with the lit match,
but I make another grab
and the smoking book falls to the floor.

We both reach for it
and just as my fingers grace the cover,
feel the etched woman on the leather,
my mother slaps me back hard onto my ass.

The Christmas bracelet rattles to the floor,
but as I breathe near the door, my cheek stinging,
all I can do is watch the pages burn.

And as she recites Scripture
words tumble out of my mouth too,
all of the poems and stanzas I've memorized spill out,
getting louder and louder, all out of order,
until I'm yelling at the top of my lungs,
heaving the words like weapons from my chest;
they're the only thing I can fight back with.

Verses

"I'm where the X is marked,
I arrived battle ready—"

> "Dios te salve, María,
> llena eres de gracia;"

"I am the indication,
I sign myself across the line."

> "el Señor es contigo;
> bendita tú eres
> entre todas las mujeres,"

"The X I am
is an armored dress
I clothe myself in every morning."

> "y bendito es el fruto
> de tu vientre, Jesús."

"My name is hard to say,
and my hands are hard, too.
I raise them here

to build the church of myself.

This X was always an omen."

"Santa María, Madre de Dios,

ruega por nosotros, pecadores,

ahora y en la hora de nuestra muerte.

Amén."

Burn

Mami stares at me like I'm speaking in tongues
and continues praying.

We're wild women, flinging verses at each other
like grenades in a battlefield, a cacophony of violent poems—

and then we're both gasping, wordless.

Tears roll down our cheeks,
but mine aren't from the smoke.
I cough on my own tongue.
I've never mourned something dying
before this moment.

I have no more poems. My mind blanks.
A roar tears from my mouth.
"Burn it! Burn it.
This is where the poems are," I say,
thumping a fist against my chest.

"Will you burn me? Will you burn me, too?
You would burn me, wouldn't you, if you could?"

Where There Is Smoke

I'm not sure when Papi and Twin tuned in
but I feel Twin rush past me;
he reaches for the notebook
but Mami hisses at him to step back
and stomps on the smoking pages.

Papi is in the room.
He speaks softly to my mother,
saying her name over and over,
"Altagracia, Altagracia."
When he reaches for the book,
she hisses at him too,
but he is soft with her,
approaching a frothing pit bull,
he bends and grabs the book by a corner and tugs.

When she lets go, he knocks it against the wall,
trying to put out the burning leather,
yells at Twin to get the fire extinguisher.

Can a scent tattoo itself onto your memory?
That's a mixed metaphor, isn't it?
My notebook is smoldering,
my heart feels like it's been burned crisp,
and all I can think about are mixed metaphors.

Things You Think About in the Split Second Your Notebook Is Burning

If I were on fire
who could I count on
to water me down?

If I were a pile of ashes
who could I count on
to gather me in a pretty urn?

If I were nothing but dust
would anyone chase the wind
trying to piece me back together?

Other Things You Think About in the Split Second Your Notebook Is Burning

I will never
write a single
poem
ever again.

I will never
let anyone
see my full heart
and destroy it.

My Mother Tries to Grab Me

Papi snatches the extinguisher from Twin
and puts out the small fire.
My mother has been standing behind the blaze,
but as the puff of dry chemicals rises between us
my knees know where she will lead me
the moment the air clears.

I scramble backward into the hallway,
push up to my feet
and away from her hands.

I stand up to my full height.
And I'm glad I'm still
wearing my coat and backpack,
because I need to leave.

I rush to the door,
turn to see Twin pulling my mother back.
She has her arm raised: a machete
        ready to cut me down.

I take the stairs two at a time.
And when I am finally outside
I breathe in—

I have nowhere to go
and nothing left.

Returning

Twin begins texting me immediately.
But I don't answer.

When I finally reply to a text
it's one I received two months ago.

X: Hey Aman. I need to talk.
Can you chill?

On the Walk to the Train

I call Caridad.
And she answers singing "Happy Birthday,"
but cuts herself off early.
"What's wrong, Xio? Are you crying?"

All I said was "Hey."
But she knows by my voice
my world is on fire.

I take a breath.
She tells me to come over.
She tells me she'll meet me.
She asks me what I need.

"Check on Twin.
Make sure he's okay.
I just need to breathe.
I just need to leave."

There's a long pause.
And I can imagine her nodding
through the phone.

"I'm here for you.
You'll figure it out."

And that's enough.

The Ride

The train stops and starts
like an old woman with a bad cough.
But I feel more than jumbled
when I walk on, so a halting train
doesn't faze me at all.

When I get off on 168th
it's started snowing softly.
I turn my face up into the wetness.
I pretend this is like a movie
where the sky offers healing.
But it only makes me colder.

I stand there waiting.
Knowing he said he would come.
Believing he will.

A tingle on my neck
is the only clue I have
and then I smell him,
his cologne a cloud
of so many memories
I didn't even know we'd made.

Aman's fingers reach
for my hand but he's silent.

I keep my face open to the sky.
I squeeze his hand in mine.

No Turning Back

Aman asks me questions
but I barely hear any of them.

The only thing I feel
is the warmth of his fingers.

We walk nowhere for a while.
Until I notice: Aman is shivering.

I finally look at him.
Really look at him.

His hair is wet, his eyelashes
have droplets from the snow,

and he is wearing nothing
but a thin hoodie.

I can see his bare ankles below his sweats—
he must have rushed out without putting on socks.

I tug on his hand, and whisper against his cold cheek:

"You're cold. Let's get out of the cold.

You live near here, right?"

And although he raises both his perfect eyebrows
there is nothing left to say.

Taking Care

The long way up five flights of stairs
I have all the silence and time to think.

I know that Aman's father works nights.
That at night Aman listens to music and does homework.

And I almost laugh.
All the time we were together and happy I avoided coming here.

And now that I'm nothing but a hot mess
I push my way into his home.

His couch is soft. Brown and cushiony.
No plastic covering like mine.

I don't take my coat off. Or my backpack.
I just lean my head back and close my eyes.

I can hear Aman moving around me.

A table leg scrapes against the hardwood floor.
The refrigerator door opens and closes softly.

Then music playing.
But not J. Cole like I expected.

Not hip-hop at all.
Instead, it's bass strings and soft steel drums.

Soca, I think, but slow and soothing.
When Aman tugs on my boots, I finally open my eyes.

And he is bending over my feet.
Staring at my mismatched socks.

Then he's sitting beside me.
And I finally begin to feel warm.

He doesn't ask what happened.
But the question floats like a blimp across the arch of his brows.

And so, I tell him all of my poems,
my words, my thoughts, the only place

I have ever been my whole self,
are a pile of ashes.

And smoke must still be lodged in my chest,
because it hurts so much when I'm done speaking.

Aman doesn't say a word;
he just pulls me to him.

In Aman's Arms

In Aman's arms I feel
warm.

In Aman's arms I feel
safe.

In Aman's arms he
apologizes.

In Aman's arms I
apologize.

In Aman's arms I want
to forget.

In Aman's arms my
mouth finds his.

In Aman's arms my
hands touch skin.

In Aman's arms my shirt
comes off.

In Aman's arms I am
shy for a moment.

In Aman's arms I am
b e a u t i f u l b e a u t i f u l
beautiful.

In Aman's arms I feel
beautiful.

In Aman's arms my
jeans unsnap.

In Aman's arms I show
myself.

In Aman's arms naked
skin rubs against mine.

In Aman's arms kisses
and kisses. My neck and ear.

In Aman's arms fingers
touch my breasts.

In Aman's arms I stop
breathing.

In Aman's arms I feel
good. So good.

And I Also Know

We have to stop.
Because now we're lying on the couch
and he's on top of me.

And his kisses feel so good,
everything feels so good.
But I also feel him pressed against me.
The part of him that's hard.
That's still an unanswered question
I don't have a response for.

And when his hand brushes my thigh
and then moves up—

I know why island people cliff dive.
Why they jump to feel free, to fly,
and how they must panic for a moment
when the ocean rushes toward them.

I stop his hand. I pull my face from his kiss.
He is breathing hard. He is still kissing me hard.
He is still bumping up against me. Hard.

"We have to stop."

Tangled

Sometimes I wear these really long three-strand necklaces.
And I love how they look. Like a spiderweb of fake gold.
But they're the worst to put away.

The next time I try to wear them they're a tangled knot.
No beginning, no end, just snag after snag.
That's how I feel the moment I ask Aman to back up.

Like a big tangle. I feel: guilty, because he looks so
frustrated. I feel: hot and wanting. I feel: like crying
because everything is so mixed up. And I feel

the panic slowly die, because I can think.
I just need a moment, things to slow down,
so I can undo the knots inside me.

The Next Move

I wait for him to call me all the names
I know girls get called in this moment.

I sit up and hold my bra against my chest
with no memory of how I became undone.

When his fingers brush against my spine
my whole body stiffens. Waiting.

But he only pulls my straps up and
snaps my bra closed. Hands me my T-shirt.

We are silent as I get dressed.
I wait for him to hand me my boots.

To point me toward the door.
I know this is how it works. You put out or you get out.

So I am surprised when instead of my boots
Aman hands me his own T-shirt,

and when I look at him confused
he takes it back and uses the sleeve

to wipe the tears sprinting down my cheek.

There Are Words

That need to be said
but we don't say any of them.

We watch YouTube highlights of the Winter Games.
I help Aman fry eggs and sweet plantains.

I sip a Malta. Aman drinks a bottle
of his father's Carib beer.

Somewhere in New York City it is late.
But in Aman's living room time has stopped.

I'm dozing off, with the lights dark
and the buzz of the computer.

With Aman's soft breathing in my ear,
I think of all the firsts I've given to this day,

and all the ones I chose to keep.
And this is a better thought

than the one that wants to break through
because in the back of my head I know

today I've made decisions
I will never be able to undo.

Wednesday, January 9
Facing It

When I walk into first-period English
Ms. Galiano takes one look at me
and stands up from her desk, gestures me outside.

Aman offered me one of his T-shirts,
but my boobs pulled it too tight across my chest
and so I'm wearing the same outfit as yesterday.
And by the way she looks at me
I know that Ms. Galiano knows it.

But she doesn't mention clothes;
she says she called my house.

That when I ran out of poetry club she got concerned,
got the number from the school directory,
that she spoke to my father, who sounded frantic,
that my whole family was wondering where I was.

She asks me if I've called them.
She asks me what's going on.
And my chest is heaving.

Because I don't know what to tell her.
She puts a soft hand on my arm

and I look into the face of a woman
not much older than me,
a woman with a Spanish last name,
who loves books and poetry,
who I notice for the first time is pretty,
who has a soft voice and called my house
because she was worried
and the words are out before I know it:

confirmation, lying about poetry, the rice,
the book burning, leaving the house, sleeping at Aman's.

My face burns hot, and the words are too fast,
and I wonder again and again why I'm saying them,
and if people are looking; but I can't seem to stop
all the words that I've held clenched tight,
and then I say words I've never even known I've thought:

"I hate her. I hate her. I hate her."

And I'm saying them against Ms. Galiano's small frame,
her slim arms around me as she hugs me tight.
As she tells me over and over:

"Just breathe. Just breathe.
It's going to be okay. Just breathe."

"You Don't Have to Do Anything You Don't Want to Do."

And so I take a breath
I didn't realize I needed to take.
When has anyone ever said those words to me?
Maybe only Aman, who's never forced me
to smoke, or kiss, or anything.

But everyone else just wants me to do:
Mami wants me to be her proper young lady.
Papi wants me to be ignorable and silent.
Twin and Caridad want me to be good so I don't attract
    attention.
God just wants me to behave so I can earn being alive.

And what about me? What about Xiomara?
When has anyone ever told me
I had the right to stop it all
without my knuckles, or my anger,
with just some simple words.

"But you do have to talk to your mom.
Really talk to her. And you do need to figure out
how to make a relationship with her work."

What I Say to Ms. Galiano After She Passes Me a Kleenex

Okay.

Going Home

Is one of the hardest things I've ever done.
All day I've been unfocused. Unsure of what I need to do.

Of how to do it. Hands trembling at the thought
of what will happen when I walk through the front door.

Because my mother's ears are soundproof when it comes to me.
The only one she ever listens to is God.

During lunch, Isabelle doesn't ask what happened,
she just hands me her bag of Doritos.

After bio, Aman rubs my shaking hands as we walk out the door.
His gentle hold warms me up.

During last period, Ms. Galiano comes to my math classroom
and gives me a note with her personal cell number in case I need to
      talk to her later.

When I step out of school, Aman's hand in mine,
both Caridad and Twin are standing at the front gate.

And although none of them can face Mami for me,
I know I'm not alone.   And I finally know who might help.

Aman, Twin, and Caridad

I introduce Aman to Twin and Caridad
before we all walk to the train station.

I want to ask Twin what happened
after I left last night.

But I don't want to know.

I can tell by how tired he looks
that whatever it was, it wasn't good.

No one says anything for a long time.

Caridad squeezes my hand and tells me to call her.
Aman kisses my forehead and tells me "we gon' be all right."

When Twin catches me looking at him
he gives me a soft smile.

And then his eyes begin to water.
On that rocking train, we hug and rock, too.

Divine Intervention

I make a stop
before going home.
Because I know
assistance comes
in mysterious ways
and I'm going to need
all the help I can get.

Homecoming

At the apartment door, I slide the key in,
but don't unlock.
I can hear both people behind me breathing.

Mami might not be home yet.
I still have time to gather my thoughts.

To get my life together.
But when I open the door
she is there. Standing in the kitchen,
wringing a dishrag. Her eyes are red.

And she looks small, so small.
Twin gives my shoulder a squeeze
and moves behind me.

I take a deep breath and square my shoulders.

"Mami, we need to talk.
And I think we need help to do it."

I step aside and let Father Sean cram into the kitchen.
He reaches out a hand to my mother: "Altagracia."

And this woman I've feared,
this woman who has been both mother and monster,
the biggest sun in my sky—
bright, blinding, burning me to the wick—

she hunches her shoulders and begins to sob.

Silent, silent crying that shakes her whole body.
And I am stuck, and still.

Before I go to her.

My Mother and I

Might never be friends.
Will never shop for a prom dress together
and paint designs on each other's nails.

My mother and I
might never learn
how to give and accept
an apology from the other.
We might be too much
the same mirror.

But our arms can do
what our words can't just now.
Our arms can reach.
Can hug tight.

Can teach us
to remember each other.

That love can be a band:
tears if you pull it too hard,
but also flexible enough
to stretch around the most chaotic mass.

My mother does not say she is sorry.
That she loves me.
And I hope one day for the words,
but for now, her strong pat on my back,
her hand through my hair,
this small moment of soft.
Is enough.

Stronger

In bio we learn about erosion.
About how over time a small stream of water
falling down the same rock face for centuries
can break an entire mountain apart
little bit by little bit.

For the next couple of weeks,
my mother and I work to break down
some of the things that have built up between us.
We meet with Father Sean once a week
and talk. Sometimes about each other.

Sometimes just about our days.
My mother starts teaching Communion classes,
and she seems happier than I've ever seen her.
The little kids make her smile, she gets excited
over teaching certain passages, and I remember
it used to be like that with me once.

It's a sweet memory made sweeter when
at the third session with Father Sean,
she gives me my name bracelet back,
the gold melded where it'd been broken, but still whole.

Sometimes Twin and Papi come to the sessions
with Father Sean. Twin wiggles uncomfortably
in his chair. I know there's a lot he doesn't say.
But I hope, one day, he will be able to say it.

Papi, surprisingly, loves to talk. And once he gets going
he makes all of us laugh, and when we are talking about him
and the things he's done that have hurt us, he doesn't leave.
He listens.

One day, as we're all leaving Father Sean turns to me
and I brace myself, afraid he is going to ask about confirmation,
and that's still a can of worms I ain't fishing with,
but instead he says:

"Xavier told us you're performing in a poetry competition.
Your very own boxing ring, eh?
I assume we're all invited?"

Slam Prep

Ms. Galiano wouldn't let me back out.
Even with everything going on,
she said I needed to give it a chance.

So, I practiced in front of my mirror
and at poetry club.

Although I lost so many poems,
and I feel a pang every time I think about them burning,
I'm also so proud of all I remember.
I'm trying to convince myself rewriting means
the words really mattered in the first place.

I need one really strong poem and although I hate
the idea of being judged and scored . . .
I love the idea of people listening.
(And, of course, winning.)

But, the thing is, all my poems are personal.
Some of the other slammers,
I know they write about politics and school.

But my poems? They're about me.
About Twin and Papi, about Aman.

344

About Mami.

How can I say things like that in front of strangers?
In house stays in house, right?
"Wrong," Ms. Galiano tells me.

She tells me words give people permission
to be their fullest self. And aren't these the poems

I've most needed to hear?

Ms. Galiano Explains the Five Rules of Slam:

1. All poems must be under three minutes

2. All work must be the poet's original work

3. You are not allowed to use props or costumes

4. You are not allowed to perform with someone onstage

5. You are not allowed to use a musical instrument

Xiomara's Secret Rules of Slam:

1. Do not faint onstage

2. Do not forget your poem onstage

3. Do not stumble over words or visibly mess up onstage

4. Do not give a disclaimer or introduction to your poem

5. Do not walk offstage without finishing the poem

The Poetry Club's Real Rules of Slam:

1. Perform with heart

2. Remember why you wrote the poem

3. Go in with all your emotions

4. Tell the audience all of the things

5. Don't suck

Friday, February 1
Poetic Justice

One week before the slam
Twin, Mami, and Papi sit on the couch.
I take a deep breath and try not to fidget.
I open my mouth

and silence.
I can't do this. I can't perform
in front of them.

The living room feels too small;
they're too close to me.
The words shrivel up and hide under my tongue.

Twin gives me an encouraging nod,
but I can tell that even he's nervous
about how my parents might react.

I close my eyes
and feel the first words of the poem
unwrinkle themselves,

expand in my mouth,
and I let them loose
and the other words just follow.

The room feels too small,
the eyes all on me,
and I take a step back

but continue staring at the wall,
at the family portrait
hanging over Papi's head.

When I'm done Twin is smiling.
When I'm done Papi claps.
When I'm done Mami cocks her head

and says:

"Use your hand gestures a little less
and next time, en voz alta.
Speak up, Xiomara."

The Afternoon of the Slam

Aman and I go to the smoke park.
I don't tell him I'm nervous
but he still holds my hand in his,
slips an earbud into my ear,
and plays Nicki Minaj.

When the album is done,
I get up to leave
but he tugs my hand
and pulls me onto his lap.

"I'm going to crush you!"

He smiles at me.
"Never, X. I have a present for you."

And I see his phone
has gone from
the iTunes app to the Notes app.

I'm stunned when he begins
reading a poem to me.

It's short and not very good
but I still blink away tears.

Because after all the poems
I've written for him and others
this is the first poem ever written for me.

"I'll never be as good of a poet as you, Poet X,
and I believe you're strong enough
to defend yourself and me at the same time,

but I'll always have your back,
and I'll always protect your heart."

And I've never heard something
more deserving of a perfect ten.

At the New York Citywide Slam

With Ms. Galiano's assistance: I let the poem rise from my heart,

With Twin helping me practice: I hand it over like a present I've had gift wrapped,

With a brand-new notebook: I perform like I deserve to be there;

With Aman's (and J. Cole's) inspiration: I don't see the standing ovation,

With YouTube and English class: I don't see Caridad and Isabelle cheering, or

With Caridad holding my hand: Aman and Twin dapping each other up,

With Mami and Papi in the front row: I don't see Father Sean in his collar smiling,

With Father Sean in the audience: I don't see Papi telling people "Esa es mi hija."

With Isabelle and the club cheering: I look at Mami and I give her a nod:

I stand on a stage and say a poem. There is power in the word.

Celebrate with Me

After the slam,
Mami and Papi
invite my friends over
and Ms. Galiano and Father Sean, too.

Mami makes rice and beans
and orders pizza,
a strange mix
but I don't complain.

Mami and Papi
won't call Aman
my boyfriend
but they let him sit on the couch.

At one point,
Isabelle starts playing
bachata on her phone
and pulls Caridad to dance with her.

Next to me,
I see Twin tap his feet
and pretend not to look at Stephan.
Aman starts Spotify DJing.

Ms. Galiano and Father Sean
begin a heated convo about Floyd Mayweather,
and then there's a tap
on my shoulder

and I turn to see Papi,
holding his hand out to me,
reaching for my arm,
asking me to dance.

"I should have taught you
a long time ago.
Dancing is a good way
to tell someone you love them."

I catch Mami's eyes in the doorway
of the living room; she smiles at me and says:
"Pa'lante, Xiomara.
Que para atrás ni para coger impulso."

And she's absolutely right,
there will be no more backward steps.
And so I smile at them both
and step forward.

Assignment 5–First and Final Draft

Xiomara Batista

Monday, March 4

Ms. Galiano

Explain Your Favorite Quote

"The unfolding of your words gives light;

it gives understanding to the simple."—Psalm 119:130

I was raised in a home of prayers and silence and although Jesus
preaches love, I didn't always feel loved. The weird thing about
the Bible is that almost everything in it is a metaphor. So it seems
to me that when the Bible describes church as a place where two
or more people discuss God, it doesn't mean just the
cathedral-like churches. I don't know what, who, or where God is.
But if everything is a metaphor, I think he or she is a comparison
to us. I think we are all like or as God.

I think when we get together and talk about ourselves,
about being human, about what hurts us, we're also talking
about God. So that's also church, right? (I know this might
seem blasphemous, but my priest tells me it's OKAY to ask
questions . . . even if they seem bizarre.) And so, I love this quote
because even though it's not about poetry, it IS about poetry. It's
about any of the words that bring us together and how we can
form a home in them. I don't know if I'll ever be as religious as

my mother, as devout as my brother and best friend. I only know that learning to believe in the power of my own words has been the most freeing experience of my life. It has brought me the most light. And isn't that what a poem is? A lantern glowing in the dark.

Acknowledgments

Writing a book can be a lonely endeavor, but I am lucky that my tribe held me up and held me close as I attempted to figure out how to tell this story.

Ammi-Joan Paquette—you the realest agent. Thank you for cheerleading me from the sidelines. I am honored be a part of the EMLA family.

To my editor, the OG of kid lit, Rosemary Brosnan, and her wonderful assistant, Courtney Stevenson, thank you for making such a caring home for me and this book at HarperCollins. I'll be forever grateful for the unwavering enthusiasm of my Harper-Collins team, who made my manuscript pages into this gorgeous book.

Special thanks to the writing mentors and peers in my life who selflessly lifted the curtain into writing and told me, "Welcome, comadre." Kayla Gatalica, Safia Elhillo, Yahaira Castro, Jason Reynolds, Ibi Zoboi, Laurie Halse Anderson, Daniel José Older, Hache Carrillo, Phil Bildner, and Kevin Lewis, thank you. Special thanks to Meg Medina for her supreme kindness and Justina Ireland for her thoughtful blurb.

I have been beyond blessed with the educators in my life. Two teachers especially stand out: Phil Bildner, I have to thank you again. You've been telling me my words mattered since I was twelve and you never failed to help me shine. This book would not exist without your encouragement. Abby Lublin, the Live Poets Society lives on, and now it lives here. Thank you for not letting a hard-headed fourteen-year-old back out of her first poetry slam. Isn't it amazing what a gentle shove can do?

Salute to the Drawbridge Collective: no matter how nervous every new leap makes me, you remind me you'll help me land on my feet. To the organization that got me involved in poetry slams as a teen, Urban Word NYC, thank you for never letting me believe any stage was too big. And special shout-out to Mahogany Browne at UW: you've continued to broaden what I imagine is possible within this work. To the Brotherhood/Sister Sol, you all were a home I needed at the time I needed it most. Lyrical Circle, thank you for the refuge you've offered for over fifteen years. The Live Poets Society of the Beacon School 2002–2006, wepa! To my former students at Buck Lodge Middle School, thank you for your patience with a new teacher and for inspiring me to write for you. And to the DC Youth Slam Teams 2013–2016: I was privileged to be your coach, and I hope this novel honors you.

To my homegirls: the Roomies, and the Love Jones Girls, and my Sigma Lambda Upsilon Hermanas (especially AG), you've heard me talk about this book for AGES but never played me like Stewie Griffin does Brian. Y'all the real MVPs.

To Carid Andrea Santos, thank you for letting me borrow your name. For reading the first rough, rough draft of this and urging me to tell the story of our home and family and childhood. For being my best best friend for the last twenty-five years. Most important, thank you for always knowing when I'm crying without my having to say a word . . . and for keeping me cute.

To my extended family, may we always celebrate together. Shout-out to my brothers, who helped me practice poems and let me keep the bedroom light on late at night to write. Thank you to my pops, who always dances with me at the Christmas party and keeps me laughing. And the absolute most special thanks to my first love, Mami, Rosa Acevedo, who took me to the library every week, taught me to read in a language she barely spoke, and showed up to every one of my poetry slams: you have prayed for every good thing that has ever happened to me and prayed yourself powerful in the face of every bad thing that has ever happened to you. Te quiero.

Beloved, Shakir Amman Cannon-Moye, I can't recall a dream I've ever whispered that you didn't believe I could manifest. Including this one. You're a better partner than I could have ever imagined, a better man than I could ever hope to write.

I want to give thanks to all the loyal folks who have followed my poetry from the early days and have now followed me on this new journey. This is for us.

Ancestors: you crossed the harshest of waters / & waters & waters / & on the other side / still gasping / your breath / dreamt us / out of the tide / & we rise / because of / for you.